Mid-Century Remodel

* * * * *

Jolene R. Whitten

First Edition

ISBN-13: 978-1548077259
ISBN-10: 1548077259

This book is dedicated to all the "Charlottes" out there, making a real difference in children's lives. There really are angels among us.

ACKNOWLEDGMENTS

I am very grateful to those who helped improve this story through the tedious process of proofreading my rough drafts. Their suggestions were invaluable. My sister, Tanya Satre DaCosta has spent a lifetime being supportive of me, and once again, she came through for me – finding mistakes, making suggestions, and thankfully, pointing out the parts she especially liked. My stepmother, Annette Satre, made time to read and offer suggestions, while facing challenges of her own – thank you, Annette.

My book club friends from Red River Unitarian Universalist Church have offered encouragement and advice, particularly Carolyn Cameron and author, Marion Moore Hill. As a new author, I greatly appreciate the guidance of fellow bibliophiles.

Two dear friends exemplify the spirit of Charlotte and inspired me to create this character: Christina Burt, by dedicating her life to the protection of children, and Deana Lane, by becoming a mom to a child who really needed one. Both have served as role models for me.

While working on this book, I experienced a great loss when my mom, Margaret Trotter passed away. I admit to being ignorant about just how devastating the loss of a mother can be, until experiencing it myself. I miss Mom more than I could ever express in words. I attribute my love of books to Mom and Dad, who read to me when I was a child, took me to the library, and were as patient as possible even while telling me to "please get your nose out of that book and come set the damned table!"

As I reflect on this story I've written, and what I've gone through the past four months after Mom's death, I realize and appreciate more than ever, the impact of a supportive and loving family. Mine includes my husband, Randy Whitten and our daughter, Mallory Whitten; my dad and stepmom, George and Annette Satre; and my sisters, Gloria Roberts and Tanya Satre DaCosta plus my precious nieces, nephew, great-nephew, aunts, uncles, cousins and all of the "significant others." No family is perfect, but I love mine, just as it is.

MID-CENTURY REMODEL

Chapter 1

Charlotte Tilian took another sip of her rum and coke and pushed the button again on the slot machine. Nothing. She'd been sitting at this same machine now for almost an hour and was down about fifty dollars, which wasn't terrible. Dottie, the waitress who'd been supplying her with her drinks this evening approached again.

"You ready for another drink, Charlie?"

Charlotte shook her head. Why had she told the waitress to call her Charlie? She hadn't used the name Charlie in years. Guess she was trying to feel young again. Pretty pathetic. "Thanks, Dottie, but I'm going to head over to the restaurant and grab something to eat. You have a good night."

"Okay. You take care."

Charlotte carefully climbed off the stool. She was always unsteady anyway and the drinks hadn't helped. She sure didn't want to fall and break something, namely a hip. She made her way to the nearest restaurant in the casino and the hostess led her to a booth.

As Charlotte took her seat, the hostess handed her a menu and told her the waitress would be right over. Charlotte picked up the menu and tried to find something that looked appetizing. Nothing sounded good. The aforementioned waitress came by and took her drink order – black coffee and a glass of water. Charlotte set the menu down and closed her eyes. What the hell was she doing? She should be back in Houston, behaving herself, instead of sitting in this Lake Charles casino, wasting her money and drinking way too many rum and cokes. But then again, what difference did it make? She heard the waitress approach her table and opened her eyes.

"Ready to order, hon?"

"Sure. Just one egg, over easy and toast, please."

"White or wheat?"

What the hell, might as well throw caution to the wind – "White."

The waitress nodded and walked off. Charlotte looked at her watch. She still had another hour before her tour bus group would leave for Houston, plenty of time to eat and sober up a little. Good lord, she was too old for this! She'd be celebrating her seventieth birthday next year. She hadn't had anything stronger than coffee in twenty-six years. She remembered, because it was on her oldest daughter's twenty-first birthday. She'd embarrassed Julie with her behavior; hell, she'd embarrassed herself. So, after years of being a horrible drunk, she'd just quit. It hadn't been easy, but she'd been determined to turn her life around and finally be a decent person. Her youngest, Heather, was fifteen at the time and she had hoped it wasn't too late to be a mother to at least one of her children. She recognized now how foolish that was — she'd been about fifteen years too late, right?

She sighed. Well, nobody left to embarrass now, was there? Just herself, and she didn't care enough about what others thought anymore to be able to embarrass herself. The waitress came over and refilled her coffee cup and Charlotte took another sip of coffee. Damn, her head hurt. She searched through her handbag but didn't find anything for the headache. She called the waitress back over and asked for the check.

"Also, is there a shop nearby where I can get some aspirin or Tylenol?"

"Sure, right around the corner. But we've got some little packets up at the counter. Want me to get you one?"

"Please."

"I think we've got Tylenol and Aleve."

"Tylenol, I guess."

"Sure thing. Be right back."

After taking the Tylenol and paying her bill, Charlotte made a stop in the ladies' room, then made her way to the front doors of the casino. She stepped outside and was hit by the hot, humid Louisiana air, though it was two-thirty in the morning. She looked around for a bench so she could sit and wait a while for the bus, which was leaving at three. One of the valet guys walked over and asked if she needed her car.

"No, thank you. I didn't drive. Do you know where the tour busses are? Mine is supposed to leave at three."

"Yes, ma'am, it should pull up right over there." He turned and pointed to an area about a hundred yards away.

"Oh. I was hoping it would pull up here."

"No, ma'am. Do you need some help? You don't look like you feel very well."

"I don't. I have a horrible headache."

"Here, let me help you over to this bench. Just have a seat for a little bit, then we'll get you over to the bus, okay? I need to go get a car for another customer, but I'll have plenty of time to help you to the bus."

"Oh, thank you so much. You're very kind."

Before the young man turned away, though, Charlotte had the strangest feeling come over her. She felt weak and confused and as she tried to talk, she found she couldn't form the words she was thinking. She felt like she was slipping. The young man broke her fall before she hit the ground and she heard someone call out, "Call nine-one-one!"

Chapter 2

So, that was six months ago. She'd been rushed to a local hospital in Lake Charles, where it was determined she'd had a stroke. After a few days, she'd been discharged from the hospital and her son, John, had come and picked her up and drove her home to Houston. He told her she couldn't keep her Houston condo and arranged for her to move into an assisted living facility. She wasn't happy about leaving her condo, but was really in no position to argue. She needed quite a bit of help at first. As far as retirement communities go, she knew she could be faced with much worse. She had a one-bedroom apartment on the second floor and there were various levels of care available to her. John even moved some of her own furniture into the apartment for her. She still had unpacked boxes in the bedroom but at least she hadn't had to give up all her belongings. Her condo was now up for sale and John said he'd come back later and help her empty it completely.

He stayed with her for a couple of weeks while she recuperated a bit and started her physical therapy. Thank goodness, the doctors in Louisiana hadn't said anything to John about her drinking; at least, she didn't think they had. She was certain he would've lectured her about it, if he'd known. Anyway, it was nice to have him around for a little while but then he headed back to that dimwit, Marlene, and their Panama City condo.

Now, here she was, sitting in the atrium of this wonderful little retirement community where John had dumped her. How she hated it here! Nothing but old people, puttering around, playing bingo, sharing photos of grandchildren, and wearing the most god-awful clothes. Seemed like their favorite activities were attending church and watching FOX News, neither of which interested her in the least. But she'd promised John she would try to get along with the other residents and even try to form some friendships. That's why she was sitting here now, in this atrium, when all she really wanted to do was head back to her room and lie down.

She noticed two women sitting across the way, deep in conversation. One of them looked in her direction, said something to the other, and looked as if she might get up and approach Charlotte. Shit! She grabbed her cell phone out of her sweater pocket and pretended to answer a call. She smiled at the woman, pointed at her phone, and shrugged and smiled as if to apologize for the interruption. The woman smiled back at her and returned to her conversation with her friend. Phew! That was close. As Charlotte pretended to end her call and return her phone to her pocket, the thing actually went off, indicating she really did have a call. The two women looked back in her direction. They were probably wondering why they hadn't heard the first call. Oh, well, who cares?

Charlotte took the call; it was her youngest, Heather. "Hello?"

"Mom! Hi. How are you feeling today?"

"Ornery."

Heather laughed. "Well, that's good. That means you're back to normal."

Charlotte smiled in spite of herself. Heather was now forty-one and the two of them had grown quite close over the years. She was the only one of the three children who wasn't perpetually angry with her. Not that she could blame John or Julie; she'd hate her, if she was them. She'd done what she could to make things up to them, but some things just can't be undone, can they?

"So, what are you up to? How are the fur babies?"

"Oh, you know. Busy, busy, as usual. Ariana has a big case she and her partners have been working on for a few weeks. I'll be glad when it's settled, she's working way too hard. And me – well, things are going good. We start filming next week. And the fur babies are fat and happy, as usual. Sunning on the patio as we speak."

Heather was a producer of documentaries, and quite successful. Her partner, Ariana was an attorney. They'd been together for about five years now and seemed to have a nice life together in L.A.

5

Their little bungalow wasn't too far from the beach and they'd often take their two little dogs there to run around. Charlotte's only gripe was that she didn't get to see Heather as often as she'd like. In fact, all three of Charlotte's children were spread out over the country. Julie was single, and lived in Denver above a tea shop that she co-owned and managed. She rarely had a day off so it had been over three years since Charlotte had seen her. John had lived in Houston where he was a bank loan officer, but he retired early and he and his new wife moved to Florida. He had children from his first marriage but they had moved off to New York with their mother years ago. Charlotte had had very little contact with her grandchildren. She knew if she tried a little harder, she could probably do something about that, but she just didn't have the energy anymore to reach out to people who didn't want to hear from her.

"So, Mom, when do you think you'll be able to travel?"

"Why?"

"Well, you have a birthday coming up. There's no way we can get away now, but I had hoped you could come out here and spend some time with us. Seventy is kind of a big deal, right?"

"It's just another number."

Heather laughed. "I should've known you'd say that. So, what do you think? Are you up to a trip to L.A.? Coco and Oscar would love to see their grandma!"

"Thanks, but I don't think so. I'm still pretty weak and I have physical therapy twice a week."

"How's that going?"

"I hate it. And I still can't use my left hand, and my left foot drags when I walk. I look like a zombie."

"Well, that will improve, right?"

"I guess. Nobody seems to know."

"Well, if you can't make it out here, we can probably come out there but it'll be a few weeks, at least."

"That's fine."

"You won't be alone on your birthday, will you? Will John be there?"

"No, I told John not to come back; he was just here, visiting, last week."

"Well, I'm sure Julie won't travel. What about friends?"

"Oh, sure. I have lots of friends. I suspect they're planning a surprise party for me. "

"So, have you made some new friends there?"

"Of course. Everyone is very friendly."

"Okay...like who?"

"What?"

"Who are your friends?"

"Oh. Well..."

Just then, a housekeeping employee walked by and Charlotte glanced at her name tag – Debbie.

"Well, there's Debbie. She's very nice."

"What's she like?"

"Ummm...well, she's a bit younger than me. Appears to dye her hair – it's very blonde. And she's short. Has a very nice smile and seems like a very happy person."

"Okay...where's she from?"

"You know, I haven't asked her. Oh, Heather, I'd better go. They're rounding everyone up to watch a movie – I think it's a Robert Redford film, you know how I love him. You tell Ariana I said hi, okay?"

"Okay, Mom. You take care. I'll call you again in a couple of days, okay? And I hope the PT gets better."

"Me, too. Love you."

"Love you too, Mom. Bye."

Charlotte ended the call and looked up. The two women on the other bench were now gone. She reached for her walker and pulled herself up. It was difficult to maneuver with her useless left hand and dragging left foot, but she managed to make her way over to the elevator. As she stood and waited for the elevator, she glanced out the glass door at the front of the lobby and saw a young woman ride up to the building on a bicycle. She leaned it against a handicapped parking sign and chained the bike to the sign's pole. Charlotte noticed she wasn't wearing a helmet; unusual these days. As she watched, the girl squatted down and pulled a shirt out of her backpack. She put it on over the tank top she was wearing; it was the same shirt worn by the housekeeping staff. She entered the building as the elevator doors opened. Some other people were getting off the elevator, so Charlotte waited a moment before entering it. She carefully walked onto the elevator, and as the doors were closing, she saw the young woman walking by; she appeared to be much younger than most of the other employees.

Once Charlotte returned to her apartment, she was exhausted from the effort of getting there. She lay down on her couch and closed her eyes. When she awoke later, the apartment was dark. She looked over at the clock on the mantel of her fake fireplace; six-thirty. Wow, she'd slept quite a while! She sat up and reached for the walker. She'd be glad when she no longer needed it. She turned on a light and made her way to the kitchen and opened the upper cabinet to the right of her refrigerator. She pulled some glasses down onto the counter and found what she was looking for at the back of the cabinet – a bottle of sangria. She'd just have a nice glass of wine while she fixed a light dinner. She looked in the fridge but couldn't find anything appetizing. She made her way to the pantry. Soup? No. She reached for the cookie jar and pulled out two cookies. This will do.

She sat at her kitchen table and munched on the cookies and sipped the sangria. Now what? She wasn't tired or hungry. She didn't feel like writing, reading or watching TV. She got up and walked over to the French doors that opened onto her balcony. She opened the doors and, leaving the walker by the doors, made her way back to the kitchen. She grabbed her glass and cautiously walked back to the balcony without use of the walker, and set the glass on the balcony table. Then she returned to the kitchen for the bottle of sangria. Once she had the glass and the bottle on the balcony table she closed the doors behind her and sat down. She was proud of herself for managing all of that without using the walker. She'd just sit out here and watch the world go by for a while.

It was a warm evening and she had a view of the park across the street. It wasn't dark yet and there were still quite a few people enjoying the park. As she watched, she noticed the same girl she'd seen earlier, walking her bike across the street. The girl stopped at a bench where a little girl was sitting. She said something to the little girl, who stood up and reached for the older girl's hand. Charlotte watched as the girl guided her bike with one hand, and the little girl with her other. Must be her sister, thought Charlotte. What was a girl that young doing by herself in the park? Charlotte watched to see if any adults approached the girls, but none did. The girls just kept walking off and Charlotte watched them until they turned a corner and she could no longer see them.

Well. Charlotte looked at the bottle. It was less than half full. How many glasses had she had? Not enough, she decided, and poured one more. As she was sipping her wine, she could hear her phone ringing in the apartment but she made no move to get up and go answer it. Whoever it was would call back later. She dozed a little bit and when she awoke again it was dark. She sighed and stood. She looked around – where was the walker? She must have left it inside. She opened the door and noticed it right inside, next to the doors, where she'd left it. She turned and looked back at the bottle and glass on her balcony table. She'd just leave them there until morning. She closed the doors behind her and made her way back to her bedroom. She should bathe and brush her teeth but she was just too tired. She lay down on her bed, fully clothed, and glanced at the clock on her bedside table – 9:15. What an exciting life, she thought, as she drifted off to sleep.

Chapter 3

What was that awful noise? She opened her eyes and saw that it was now daylight. Glancing over at the clock on her nightstand, she saw that it was eight-thirty. There it was again – the doorbell. Who the hell was at her door at this time of day? She sighed, sat up, and smoothed out her clothes. Reaching for the walker by her bed, she pulled herself up and walked toward the bedroom door. The doorbell rang again.

"Just a minute! I'm coming!" she called out.

She got to the door and peered out the peephole. It was that young girl she'd seen yesterday. Hmmm...what could she want? Charlotte opened the door just a few inches and peered out at the girl.

"Yes?"

"Good morning, ma'am. I'm sorry if I woke you. I was told to come and clean your apartment."

"What? Really?"

"Yes, ma'am. I'm from housekeeping." She pointed to the name on her shirt. "Lexi."

Charlotte reached up to smooth her hair. She knew she must look a fright, having slept in her clothes and all. "Do you have to do it now? I mean, can you come back in a bit?"

Lexi pulled a cell phone out of her back pocket and checked the time. "Well, it's about eight-thirty." She looked back up at Charlotte. "I've got a few other apartments to clean. What time works for you?"

"Oh, just about any time. I just need a little time to straighten up the place, that's all."

"Ma'am, that's what I'm here for. You don't need to clean up your place before I come to clean it."

Charlotte couldn't help smiling. "I guess that does sound silly. Well, okay, come on in. But don't say I didn't warn you."

"Yes, ma'am. Thank you."

Charlotte opened the door further to let Lexi in, and stepped aside. Lexi grabbed a few items off the housekeeping cart just outside the door, then stepped into Charlotte's apartment. Charlotte closed the door behind her and turned back to her. "So, where do you want to start?"

Lexi looked around. "I guess in here, in the main living area."

"Good. I'll leave you to it."

Charlotte took hold of the walker and made her way back to her bedroom. She straightened up the bedcovers then went into the master bath to freshen up. She looked at her reflection in the mirror; she looked terrible but she figured a young teenager probably felt all old women looked terrible, so what did it matter? She ran a brush through her hair and washed her face. She thought about changing her clothes but then realized if she did that, Lexi would figure out that she'd slept in what she was wearing. She turned out the light and stepped back into her bedroom. She decided she'd try not to rely on the walker today, so she left it by the bed and stepped out into the living area. Lexi had opened the blinds on the French doors and Charlotte could see the wine bottle and glass were no longer on the balcony table. She made her way into the kitchen and found Lexi there, wiping down the counters. The wine glass was in the dish drainer and the bottle was on the counter, next to the coffee maker.

Charlotte walked over to the coffee maker. "I'll just make some coffee. Would you like a cup?"

"No, thank you."

"Tea? Water?"

"I'm fine, thanks. I do have a question, though."

Charlotte filled the coffee filter and picked up the carafe to fill it with water. As she was filling the carafe, she asked, "What is it?"

"Well, I dusted off the bookcases in your living area. But there's nothing on them. Did you just move in or something?"

"Oh. Well. Yes, I haven't been here that long. A few weeks. I have some books in boxes but I haven't gotten around to unpacking and putting them on the shelves yet. Maybe by the next time you come, I'll have done that."

"I could do that for you now, if you like."

"Oh, no, I couldn't ask you to do that. I know you still have other apartments to clean."

"Well, you're right, I do. How about this? I should be done cleaning by eleven-thirty. Then I'll drop back by and empty the boxes for you. I can even flatten the boxes and take them downstairs."

Charlotte thought to herself, two visits in one day? Could she be sociable enough to handle such a thing?

Lexi saw the hesitation in Charlotte. "But if today's not good for you, that's okay. I'll just build extra time into next week's schedule and do it then."

"Aren't you in school?"

"Sure. This is Saturday."

"But I've seen you here on other days."

"Yeah, in the afternoons. I work evenings and weekends."

"How old are you?"

"Eighteen."

"Eighteen."

"Yes, ma'am."

Charlotte thought she looked younger, but kept her opinion to herself.

"Are you in high school or college?"

"Senior year of high school."

"Do you drive?"

"Drive?"

"Yes. Do you drive? A car."

"Not yet. I took the written test to get my learner's permit, but I don't have my license yet. I don't have a car, anyway, so not really any point in it."

"I guess that's true. So, is that why you're working so hard? To get a car?"

"Sure. Well, speaking of working hard, I guess I'd better get back to it. So, what about the shelves?

"Oh. If you want to come back at eleven-thirty, that will be fine."

"Okay, great."

Lexi went into Charlotte's bedroom and started dusting in there. Charlotte sat down on her couch and sipped her coffee. It would be so nice to just lie down for a moment and take a little nap but she figured Lexi would wonder why she was taking a nap when she'd just gotten out of bed about twenty minutes ago. She got up and walked back into the kitchen. An idea was forming in her brain but she couldn't quite grasp it. Something about Lexi having a permit. She opened the fridge and peered inside. She knew she should eat something. Nothing looked appetizing but she grabbed a small tub of yogurt and a bottle of water and carried them to the kitchen table. As she sat down, she heard water running in her bathroom, indicating Lexi was cleaning it. A few minutes later, Lexi came out of the bedroom.

"I'm going to grab my vacuum cleaner; be right back."

"Okay."

Charlotte finished up her breakfast and tossed the yogurt container in the trash. She went back into the living room and reached for her coffee cup; it was still half full. She took a sip – cold. She took it back to the kitchen and was going to pop it in the microwave but decided she really didn't want the coffee, so just dumped it in the sink and put the mug in the dishwasher. She heard the vacuum cleaner start up, so decided she'd just sit on the balcony for a bit and stay out of Lexi's way.

She sat on the balcony and looked across at the park. She saw the same little girl that she'd assumed was Lexi's sister, sitting on the same bench, reading a book. Lexi's bicycle was propped up against the bench. There were other people in the park, too. Joggers, parents with little kids playing on the playground, a group of boys playing soccer. The little girl on the bench seemed oblivious to her surroundings, totally engrossed in her book. Charlotte wondered what she was reading

13

and how old she was. She couldn't be more than ten or eleven. Was she going to sit there all morning, while Lexi worked? What about their parents? Charlotte heard the vacuum cleaner shut off and turned to watch Lexi unplug it and carry it back outside. Then Lexi came back into the apartment and walked back toward the balcony.

"I'm through Ms. Tilian. I'll see you about eleven-thirty."

"Okay. Thank you."

Lexi turned and walked out of the apartment. Charlotte pulled herself up off her balcony chair and walked back into the apartment. She was feeling a little unsteady so made her way back to the bedroom to find the walker. When she got there, she felt so tired. She sat down on the bed. A little nap would be good. She lay back down and was soon sound asleep.

Chapter 4

Charlotte fell asleep quickly but to disturbing dreams. She started to call out but the threat remained. She opened her eyes and instantly felt relief flood over her. Thank God. It was just a dream. She sat up and looked at the clock – 9:50. She stretched and sighed. She looked over at the boxes stacked against the wall, the boxes Lexi was coming back to unload for her. It all seemed so pointless.

She could hear her cell phone ringing. Where had she left it? She got up, grabbed hold of the walker, and went into the living room. There it was, on the end table. She made her way to the phone and picked it up just as it quit ringing. She looked at the number; it was a local number but meant nothing to her. She set it down and looked around her. What now? Maybe a little sunshine would do her some good. She picked up the phone and slid it into her sweater pocket, and walked into the kitchen without benefit of the walker. She got a clean wine glass out of the cupboard and poured the remaining wine into it. She rinsed out the bottle and placed it in the recycle bin in her little pantry. She made her way to the balcony and set the glass on the table and looked across the street. She couldn't see Lexi's little sister anywhere. She settled into her chair and closed her eyes. The sun felt good on her face. It had been a long time since anything felt good, so she relished in it for a moment.

Her peace was quickly disturbed, though, by the sound of her cell phone ringing again. Sighing, she opened her eyes and fished the phone out of her pocket. It was the same person who'd called earlier. She didn't know who it was, so she ended the call without answering and placed the phone on the table. She picked up her wine glass and looked over at the park. She spotted Lexi's little sister sitting in the grass. The bike was lying on the ground next to her and the girl was searching in a backpack for something. Charlotte kept sipping her wine. As she watched, Lexi's sister pulled a candy bar from the backpack, unwrapped it and took a bite. She then turned to the backpack

15

again and pulled out a bottle of water. Charlotte continued watching the girl and sipping her wine. Then she heard the doorbell ring. Who could that be? It was too early for Lexi to be back.

She got up and went inside the apartment, leaving her wine glass and cell phone on the balcony table. The doorbell rang again. "Coming!"

She looked out the peephole. Shit! It was that damned activities director who was always pestering her to join some idiotic thing or another. Reluctantly, she opened the door.

"Yes?"

"Oh, Mrs. Tilian! I'm so happy to see you!"

"It's Ms. Tilian. What can I do for you?"

"Oh, yes, of course, of course. Miss Tilian. Sorry."

"No. Not Miss. Ms."

The woman looked puzzled. "Okay...."

"What do you need?"

"Well, I just wanted to make sure you're okay, *Mizz* Tilian. I tried calling you a couple of times but you didn't answer."

Charlotte said nothing.

The woman paused a moment, then seeing that Charlotte was not going to provide her with a reason for not answering the phone, continued: "I was calling to let you know that we're having a little gathering tonight we're hoping you can attend. The residents are starting a book club, and their first meeting is at six this evening. They'll be selecting books for the year, but mostly, it will just be a chance for everyone to get to know each other. There will be cheese and crackers and wine or iced tea, if you don't drink wine. We felt you'd surely want to join the book club and I know everyone would just be so honored if you did." She smiled a big smile.

Charlotte forced a smile back at her. "I'm very sorry, but I have other plans tonight."

"Oh. Well, that's disappointing. Is your son in town?"

"My son?"

16

"Well, you said you have plans so I just assumed he was taking you somewhere?"

"No."

The woman waited, appearing to think Charlotte would offer more information.

"I'm sorry, but I really need to go sit back down again. Still a bit weak after the stroke, you understand."

"Oh, yes, yes. I'm sorry. Forgive me for keeping you standing at the door like this. Anyway, I'm glad you're alright."

"Thank you."

Charlotte closed the door before the woman could say another word. On her way back to the balcony, she retrieved her e-reader from an end table in the living room. Maybe she'd sit and read something. She settled back down into the balcony chair and took a sip of wine. She glanced over at the park again and saw that the little girl was now lying down with her head on her backpack, her book covering her face as if to shield her eyes from the sun. So, she takes naps, too. Charlotte picked up the e-reader and selected a book she'd started months ago. She started to read but her mind kept drifting. Finally, about thirty minutes later and still on the same page, she gave up and set the e-reader down with a sigh.

She looked across the street at the park. The little girl appeared to be sound asleep. But she wasn't alone. Charlotte froze. A man was standing with his back to Charlotte, about six feet from where the little girl lay on the grass. He was looking down at the girl, then appeared to look around to see if anyone was watching him. Charlotte felt in her bones that he was a menace. She needed to do something. But what? Would the man hear her if she screamed at him? She opened her mouth to try, just as a soccer ball went hurling through the air and knocked the man in the head. Two boys, who appeared to be teenagers, came chasing after the ball. She could hear the man yell out in surprise or pain, she wasn't sure which, and the boys appeared to be apologizing. In the commotion, the girl woke, saw what was going on, and jumped up. She put the pack on her back, grabbed the bike off the ground, climbed on, and rode off toward the sidewalk. The man and the boys didn't even seem to notice the girl as they were now in a full-blown shouting match. Some other boys ran over and before long, there was quite a crowd now standing where the girl had once sat eating her candy bar. Charlotte looked back in the direction the girl had been headed but couldn't see her anywhere. She watched the boys and the man continue to gesture and yell at each other until the man turned and walked toward the parking lot. Charlotte watched him climb into a black pickup truck; she wished she could make out the license plate from here, but it was impossible. The truck pulled out of the parking lot and the boys turned away and returned to their soccer game.

Where had the girl gone? Would she be safe? Did she know that man? Had she known she was in danger? And what the hell business is it of mine? I can't do a damned thing about it anyway, stuck up here on my balcony, a helpless old woman who can't even walk for more than a few minutes without the assistance of a walker. I'm useless to her – useless to anyone. Charlotte stood up, grabbed the now empty wineglass, and made her way back into the apartment.

Chapter 5

Later that morning, the doorbell rang again. Charlotte grabbed her walker and pulled herself up off the couch. She made her way slowly across the room to the front door. At least Lexi had sense enough not to ring the bell again, apparently knowing how slowly Charlotte moved. Charlotte peered out through the peephole and verified that it was, indeed Lexi, before opening the door.

"Hi."

"Hi, Lexi. Come on in."

Lexi came in and Charlotte closed and locked the front door. "I'd offer to help you, but I'd probably be more of a hindrance, I'm sorry."

"Oh, don't worry about it. It won't take me long, then I'll get out of your hair."

"Okay. Well. You know where the boxes are. Help yourself."

"Yes ma'am."

Charlotte turned and walked back toward the French doors leading to the patio. She peered out and saw the girl, sitting on the bench again. There were two other girls sitting on the bench, too, and the three girls appeared to be chattering away, having a good time. So, she was safe. Good. No need to do anything further – what that would be, anyway, she didn't really know. She turned back and returned to the living area, sitting in a chair across the room from the bookshelves.

Lexi was kneeling in front of the shelves, with the first box opened. "Do you want these in any particular order? Alphabetized by author name, maybe? Or arranged by subject matter?"

Charlotte thought to herself, I don't think I'm even capable of making such a decision. She sighed. "Oh, it doesn't matter. Whatever you think best."

"Oh. Okay. Well, let's see what we have." She opened the box and started pulling out books. "It appears they must have been arranged alphabetically before they were packed. All of these authors' names seem to start with C through F."

"Well. Alphabetically it is, then."

She watched as Lexi arranged the books on a shelf, then folded up the box and placed it near the front door. Lexi then went back to the bedroom and returned with a second box. She opened it and reached in for a book.

"I'm in luck. This author's name starts with A."

Charlotte nodded at her and watched as Lexi unpacked the second box. Lexi appeared to be interested in the books, reading the titles as she placed the books on the shelves. She thought about the girl who appeared to be Lexi's sister, reading the book in the park.

"Do you like to read, Lexi?"

"Oh, yes ma'am. Any chance I get, I've got a book in my hands. I try to get to the library at least once a week."

"That's good. And your parents? They must be readers too?"

"Not so much. Well, that's two down, five to go." Lexi stood and placed the second flattened box on top of the first one. And so it went. Charlotte watched as Lexi unpacked each box, carefully placing the books on the shelves. She even started to doze a bit but opened her eyes as Lexi quietly asked, "Ma'am?"

Charlotte looked over at Lexi. She was holding a book, reading the back of the jacket cover. She looked up at Charlotte, questioningly. "Is this you?"

Charlotte looked at the book in question, and back at Lexi. She nodded.

"Wow. That's amazing. You're an author."

"*Was* an author."

Lexi frowned. "Why was?"

"I haven't written anything in quite a while."

"Why not?"

"Oh, I don't know. Life. Writer's block." She waved her hand as if she was swatting a fly. "Doesn't really matter why. I just don't."

Lexi looked back down at the book. "How many did you write?"

"Not a lot. I started out writing short stories, some of which were published in magazines. A few poems. Then a couple of novels."

"A couple? What was the other one called?"

"Well, more than a couple, I guess. They're all there. In that box."

Lexi looked down at the box. "Why is your last name different on this one book? Was this a pen name?"

"No. That was my first published book. It was my married name. I later changed my name. My publisher was horrified when I refused to continue using the same name. She thought it would affect sales."

"Did it?"

"Sure. At first. Then people took an interest in why I changed my name and in the end, it seemed to have helped sales. People love gossip, Lexi."

Lexi nodded. "Is Tilian your maiden name, then?"

"No."

"You remarried?"

"No."

Lexi looked puzzled but didn't ask any more questions. She started pulling out the other books and reading the titles and jacket covers. Charlotte watched as Lexi searched for the copyright year on each book, appearing to shelve them in chronological order. Smart girl. Lexi finished with that box and went back to the bedroom for the final one. As she set the final box down in front of the book case, her stomach growled. She looked up at Charlotte. "Excuse me." The girl seemed embarrassed.

Charlotte smiled. Well, this was unusual – how long had it been since she'd even felt like smiling? "Don't worry about it. I'm sure you're hungry. It's well past lunch time and you've been working hard. Do you get a lunch break?"

"No, ma'am. I usually quit by noon and eat lunch at home. In fact, I guess I'd better go clock out now and head home."

Charlotte nodded. "Wait a moment." She got up and went back to her bedroom. She found her handbag and pulled out a twenty-dollar bill. She walked back into the living room. "Here's a little tip. I really appreciate your doing this for me, Lexi." She held the money out to Lexi.

"Oh, no, that's too much. I was happy to do this, Ms. Tilian. And I don't think my supervisor would want me to accept a tip."

"It is not too much. Don't worry about it. I'm an old woman with nothing else to spend my money on. And I don't give a rat's ass what your supervisor in this damned place thinks. It's none of their business, anyway, it's between you and me. Here - take it. Maybe you and your sister can go out for lunch, have some fun."

Lexi took the twenty-dollar bill, folded it, and placed it in a back pocket of her jeans. "My sister?"

"Oh, I assume she's your sister. But maybe not. I've seen her with you. She's been in the park this morning, with a red bicycle. Curly black hair, pulled back in a ponytail?"

"Yes. That's my sister."

"Well, you two enjoy a nice lunch together. Then maybe you can go to the library this afternoon."

"No, not today. But maybe lunch. Thank you."

Lexi looked over at the bookshelves. "That looks nice. All those books. One day, I'll have a place of my own, filled with books, just like you do." She smiled over at Charlotte. "You're so lucky. I'd give anything to have your life."

"My life?"

"Yes, ma'am. Independent. Your own place. It's so peaceful here. You've written books and poetry and I'll bet you've known all kinds of people and done all kinds of things. One of these days, I'll — well, just one of these days…"

22

She picked up the flattened boxes and opened the door. "Bye, Ms. Tilian. See you around."

"Bye, Lexi."

Charlotte was too shocked to say anything else. Lucky? Lexi, this beautiful young girl with her whole life ahead of her, had referred to her as lucky. Humph. Maybe she wasn't so smart, after all.

Chapter 6

The rest of the weekend dragged along slowly. Charlotte spent much of it napping. Oh, she tried to do some reading, even turned on the TV for a little while, but her mind just would not focus on anything. She didn't seem to have the ability to concentrate, even for thirty minutes to watch a silly sitcom. And she was just so tired. It seemed like the more she rested, the more fatigued she felt. She was out of wine, and thought about making a trip to the grocery store, but she just didn't have enough energy.

On Sunday afternoon, she decided to sit out on the balcony and watch people in the park but after five minutes, she decided it was too hot outside and went back into the apartment. As she made her way to the couch, she had a call on her cell phone, which was lying on the coffee table. She glanced at it. Him again. She ignored the call and it went to voice mail. Damn, she really needed a drink. In her mind, she went through the motions of making her way down to her car, driving to the store, buying some wine, driving back, and making her way back up to her apartment. She was exhausted just thinking about it. She sat down on the couch and sighed. The phone went off again. This time it was Heather, so Charlotte took the call.

"Hello, Heather."

"Hi, Mom. How's it going?"

"Oh, you know. Another exciting day in the neighborhood. You?"

"Thankfully, no excitement. Ariana and I had a late breakfast and we're just staying home today, relaxing. It's been a busy week for both of us. So, how's Houston? Hot already?"

"It's beginning to get pretty warm, yes."

"You need to come out here and spend some time with us. We're having perfect weather right now."

"That would be nice. I just don't think I'm up to dealing with airports quite yet, though. So, tell me, what's kept you two so busy this week?"

Charlotte listened as Heather filled her in on her busy life. She was proud of Heather and so happy that Heather was happy. Heather asked if she'd heard from Julie or John lately.

"Oh, it's been awhile, I guess. Have you?"

"No. I may give them both a call today. Hopefully, Julie won't be working. I'm sure John will be out on a golf course, though, so I'll probably wait until evening."

"That's true, he does play a lot of golf."

"Well, there are worse things, I guess."

Charlotte nodded. Don't I know it, she thought.

"Okay, Mom, I guess I'll go. Ariana says hi and the fur babies send kisses."

"Can I speak with Ariana? Or is she busy?"

"Never too busy for you, Mom. Hold on."

Charlotte waited while Heather passed the phone to Ariana.

"Hey, Charlotte! How's it going, girl? You behaving?

"I don't seem to have much choice these days."

"Well, come out here and we'll see what kind of trouble we can get into. I miss my partner in crime."

Charlotte couldn't help but smile. "That would be fun, Ariana. Soon, I promise."

They talked a couple more minutes before Ariana returned the phone to Heather. "We really do miss you, Mom. When will you be done with the physical therapy?"

"I don't know, honey. I seem to have reached a plateau. Not making much progress now. I had thought I'd be done with it by now, but this old body isn't cooperating."

"Well, try to work extra hard at it so you can get better. Are you exercising at home, too?"

"Oh, sure."

"That sounded real convincing."

"Guilty, as charged. Okay, I'll try to do better."

"Good girl. Well, you take care, Mom. I love you."

"I love you, too. Bye."

"Bye."

Charlotte ended the call and placed the phone back on the coffee table. Heather was right, she should be exercising. She got up and made her way to her bedroom. She had put a printout of exercises she was supposed to do at home between therapy sessions, in her desk. She sat at the desk and opened the top drawer. And there it was. The letter. With a Philadelphia postmark, addressed to Charlotte at her old address. It had been awhile since she'd read it. She picked it up and her hand shook. Just then, she heard her phone again. She returned the letter to the drawer, closed it, and stood up. She made her way back to the living room and picked up the phone just as it quit ringing. It was him again. Damn! She tossed the phone on the couch and went back to her bedroom, but this time she lay down on the bed and buried her face in her pillow. She would *not* cry, she told herself. She tried to think of other things and took some deep breaths to calm herself. Before long, she was asleep. The only way to find some peace.

Chapter 7

Unfortunately, sleep didn't bring her the peace she sought. Instead, she had disturbing dreams involving people from her past. Finally, she woke up to the sound of her own screams. It was actually a relief to open her eyes and find herself safely in bed, in her apartment. The room was dark and she glanced at her clock – it was almost nine o'clock. Her stomach rumbled and she knew she should eat something. She sat up and reached for the walker.

In the kitchen, she opened the pantry and peered inside. She pulled out a can of tomato basil soup and the loaf of bread. She'd have soup with a grilled cheese sandwich – comfort food but not too heavy. As she prepared her meal, she remembered how it had been John's favorite lunch when he was a little boy. He'd thought it was a real treat when she made it for him. *I guess there were moments when she'd been a decent mother.* Few and far between, but hopefully enough that he had some good memories of his childhood. She sat at the kitchen table to eat her dinner and the phone started again. She'd just ignore it. She continued eating. The phone rang again. She kept eating. And it rang again.

Finally, she got up and went back to the couch. She picked up the phone. It wasn't him; it was John. She answered the phone.

"Hello."

"Mom! Are you okay? I've been calling and calling."

"I'm sorry, sweetheart. I was having a bath. I'm fine."

"Oh, good. I'm sorry, I was just worried."

"It's okay. I'm glad you care enough to worry. But I'm fine. Really."

"So, what have you been doing?"

"Well, let's see. I've finally got the last of the boxes unloaded."

"Great! You were able to do that yourself?"

"Well, probably, but I didn't. A young woman who works for housekeeping here, did it for me. By the way, have you arranged for them to clean my apartment for me?"

"Yes. They're supposed to come twice a week until you're feeling better, then once a week. That's okay, isn't it?"

"I suppose so. I feel strange, though, having someone else clean my apartment for me. I don't know how long I'll need the service, but I must admit, it's nice to have it right now."

"So, what else have you been up to? Doing any writing?"

"Oh, no. Not really. I've got some ideas rolling around in my head, but I haven't put anything down in writing, no. There's a new book club starting here, though, and they've asked me to join that. And of course, I have my physical therapy and then the exercises at home. I may start using the indoor pool they have here; that's supposed to be great exercise."

"Well, be sure someone else is with you if you decide to swim, at least the first few times."

"Oh, don't worry. I have a lot of friends here. That's not a problem."

"Well, great! It sounds like you're really settling in there. I'm glad to hear it. I'll bet you don't even miss the old place now, right?"

"You're right, John. This place is lovely. I should have sold the condo years ago. I'm glad you encouraged me to move here."

"That's what I told Heather earlier. She called me, you know. She was going on about how worried she is about you, and she thinks you're lonely and miss your old place and the old neighborhood. She's afraid you feel 'isolated' – that's the word she used. I told her she was crazy, that you're having a ball at that senior community but she wouldn't have it. She just knows you're miserable. She said she and Ariana are planning a trip to see you in a few weeks, even though they're both incredibly busy, because she's so worried about you. I told her that was nonsense but she won't believe me."

Charlotte felt a pang of guilt. She hadn't fooled Heather. She'd have to try harder. She didn't want to cause any hardship for her and Ariana.

"I'll talk to her, John. I thought she just wanted to visit to celebrate my birthday. I had no idea she was worried about me."

"Well..." John seemed to hesitate. "I'm sure that's part of it, too. She doesn't like that you'll be alone on your birthday. You won't be, though, will you? I mean, you'll have friends over, right?"

"Of course. I'll be fine. Frankly, I'd rather forget that I'm going to be seventy. Though, truthfully, there are days when I actually feel older."

"Lord, me too! Only nine holes of golf today and I'm bushed. Getting old sucks, huh? Well, Mom, guess I'll go. I just wanted to check in and make sure you're okay."

"I'm fine, John. Don't worry about me. You've settled me in a nice place and all my needs are being met. Everything's good."

"Great, Mom. That's great. Take care."

"Bye, John."

"Bye, Mom."

She ended the call and sighed. She looked through the list of missed calls, noting she'd had several while she'd slept. She deleted them, as well as the voice mail messages. Now what? She looked around. It was time most people her age went to bed, and here she was, just having slept all day and nothing to do all night. In her younger days, she would have hit the town and made a night of it. But these weren't her younger days. So, what does an old woman do when she can't sleep and has nothing to do? She looked over at the bookshelves. Maybe a good book.

She settled on the couch with a book and a cup of tea and started to read. But as usual, lately, she couldn't focus on what she was reading. After a while she gave up and set the book down. She reached for the remote and started flipping through channels. Not much on that interested her. Finally, she settled on an old movie and before long, was engrossed in the story.

Chapter 8

Several hours and three movies later, she reached for her phone to check the time but the battery had died. She got up and took it to the kitchen to charge it. The clock on the microwave said it was four a.m. She peered out the windows of the French doors. Even at this hour, Houston was awake. Lights on, streets busy with traffic. The park across the street looked quiet, though. She closed the blinds and turned toward the bedroom. She grabbed some clean clothes from the dresser and headed to the bathroom to shower. Today, she would accomplish something. She wasn't sure what yet, but something.

A little later, she was sitting at her kitchen table drinking a cup of coffee and eating a slice of toast. She heard a thump against the front door — the newspaper being delivered. She got up, looked out the peephole on the front door, and saw no one. She opened the door and looked down. Yep, the paper was on the doormat. She reached down and picked it up and noticed a man a few doors down, placing another newspaper on a neighbor's doormat. She closed and locked the front door and returned to her breakfast. By the time she finished reading the paper, it was getting light outside. She washed her coffee cup and went to the desk in her bedroom to grab a notepad. She returned to the kitchen with it and looking through the cupboards and refrigerator, determined what she needed and started making a grocery list. Wine was at the top of the list.

At nine-fifteen her doorbell rang. She answered the door and there was Jerry, the van driver. "Mornin' Ms. Tilian. You ready to roll?"

"Yes, Jerry. Ready as I'll ever be."

"D'you have a good weekend?"

"Yes, thank you. You?"

"Oh, yes ma'am. You know, typical weekend. Soccer games with the kids, yardwork. Busy, busy, busy."

"Of course. Maybe you can get some rest now that you're back at work."

Jerry laughed. "You're right about that, ma'am."

Jerry drove her to the rehab center for her physical therapy. The therapist noticed that Charlotte hadn't brought her walker today.

"You must be feeling stronger, Charlotte. No walker today, I see."

"Yes, I've been using it less and less."

"That's good, Charlotte. But I also want you to be safe. Are you sure you don't need it when you're outside your apartment, like today?"

"If I wasn't sure, I would have brought it."

"Okay, then. Well, let's get started."

An hour later, Charlotte made her way back to the lobby to wait on Jerry. He pulled up right on time, got out of the van and walked through the front doors as Charlotte stood and walked toward him.

"Hello, Jerry."

"Hello, ma'am. You ready to head back? You need to run any errands or anything?"

"Well, if you have time, I do need to get some groceries and fill a prescription. Would that be alright?"

"Sure, no problem. Randall's again?"

"Yes."

"Okay, let's go." He slid open the van's side door and helped Charlotte get into her seat. She sighed as she sat and realized she was very tired after the therapy. After Jerry started the van, she spoke up. "You know, Jerry, I think I've changed my mind. After all that exercise, I just don't think I'm up to a trip to the grocery story. Let's just go home."

"You sure, Ms. Tilian? What about that prescription? You want to at least get that? We can go through the pharmacy's drive-through."

"Well, that's probably a good idea. Okay."

So, Jerry drove to Randall's and they picked up her prescription at the drive-through window. As they drove back toward home, Charlotte closed her eyes and was soon fast asleep. Staying up all night and the physical therapy had worn her out; she napped until Jerry pulled into the parking space at the retirement community. He turned around and looked at her.

"Ms. Tilian, would you like me to get a wheelchair? You seem pretty tired."

"Oh, no thank you, Jerry. I'm fine. I just didn't sleep well last night, but I can walk back to my apartment, don't worry."

"You sure?"

"I'm sure."

"Okay, then." He got out, opened the door for her, and helped her out. He accompanied her to the elevators and as he turned to leave, she stopped him and handed him a ten-dollar bill.

"Thank you, ma'am."

"You're welcome, Jerry. Have a good day."

"You too, Ms. Tilian. See you later."

"Bye."

Once she was back in the apartment, she decided she'd take a nap so went into the bedroom and lay down. Oh, it felt good to rest. Soon, she was sound asleep.

Later in the day, she sat on the balcony and watched people in the park. Before long, she saw her again, Lexi's little sister. She was further away this time, sitting on another bench. She didn't see a bicycle anywhere near the girl today. Once again, the girl was reading.

Charlotte got up and went back into the apartment. She found what she was looking for her in her bedroom closet – her fanny pack. Though she thought it looked ridiculous, it really was the best way to carry anything she might need while using the walker, such as her keys or phone. So, she put on the fanny pack, grabbed the walker, and made her way out the front door. As she got on the elevator that damned activities director also got on.

"Why, hello, *Ms*. Tilian! How are you today?"

"Fine, thank you. And you?"

"Oh, just peachy. Headed to Bingo. Would you like to join us?"

"No, thank you. It sounds like fun but I have other plans."

"That's nice."

The elevator doors opened. "Well, have a good afternoon."

"Thanks. You, too."

Charlotte watched the insufferable woman walk off then turned the opposite direction and made her way to a bench in the lobby. She sat and waited and before long, she saw Lexi with the house-keeping cart. She got up and using the walker, made her way toward Lexi, who looked up and smiled at Charlotte.

"Hi, Ms. Tilian."

"Hello, Lexi."

"How are you?"

"Oh, fine. Did you have a nice weekend?"

"Sure, it was okay."

"Listen, I was thinking. How about a driving lesson today?"

"What? I mean, excuse me? A driving lesson?"

Charlotte nodded. "You do have your permit with you, don't you?"

"Well, yes."

"Good. What time does your shift end?"

"Five-thirty."

"Okay. We'll start at five-thirty, then."

"But, I can't. I mean…well…."

"Yes?"

Lexi looked around, as if she feared being overheard.

"Well, it's my sister. As it is, I hate that she has to wait alone for me in the park while I work. I don't want to leave her even longer, just so I can go drive, you know?"

"She can come with us."

Lexi looked at her. "You think that's a good idea? To have her with us while you're teaching me to drive?"

"Oh. I see your point. Well, she can wait in my apartment. She'd be safe there."

"Really? You wouldn't mind that?"

"Is there any reason why I shouldn't want to leave her alone in my apartment?"

"No."

"How old is she?"

"Eleven."

"Well. We may be breaking some kind of rule, leaving her alone at age eleven. But it can't be any worse than leaving her alone in a park, can it?"

"No, ma'am. She's used to being left alone, anyway. It's no big deal."

"Alright, then. You two meet me at my apartment at five-thirty."

"Why are you doing this for me?"

"I'll explain that later."

"Okay." Lexi seemed hesitant.

"Don't worry. It's nothing sinister. I just need to be able to get out and do things when I want, without having to depend on the nosey staff here, and I'm not able to drive yet. I figure this is a win-win situation. You get a driving lesson and I get out of the apartment. And you seem like the kind of person who can mind her own business."

Lexi nodded. "Okay. That makes sense. And you have a license, right? And a car?"

Charlotte smiled. "Yes and yes."

"What kind?"

"Kind?"

"Of car. It isn't a huge Cadillac or anything, is it?"

"No. Actually, it's a Prius. Small and easy to drive."

"Cool."

"See you at five-thirty."

"Okay. Thanks."

Charlotte turned and went back to the elevator.

Chapter 9

Around four-thirty, there was a knock at her door. She peered out – it was Lexi. She opened the door. "Hi. You're early."

"No, ma'am. I just dropped by to tell you I won't be here exactly at five-thirty. I mean, I get off at five-thirty. But then I'll have to check out and go get Jade. So, it may be closer to five-forty-five before we get here. Is that okay?"

"Of course. Thanks for letting me know."

"You're welcome."

Lexi turned to go and Charlotte closed the door.

So, her name is Jade. Pretty. Charlotte walked over to the French doors and looked across at the park. There she was, sitting on the bench again. She appeared to be doing homework. Charlotte looked around but didn't see any men lurking around or a black pickup like the one she saw the other day. Just kids playing, joggers, a guy throwing a frisbee for a dog. Jade seemed to be safe.

Charlotte turned back to the living room, just as her phone rang. She fished it out of her sweater pocket and looked down at the number. She ignored the call and returned the phone to her pocket. *I will not let him upset me,* she thought. *I'll just sit and think about the driving lesson I'm about to give Lexi and then she'll be here and we'll head out for the lesson. I won't even think about him.* She sat down on the couch and closed her eyes, thinking back over the years and recalling when she taught Heather to drive. She'd paid for Heather to go to a driving school so all she'd had to do was take her out driving for practice. Heather had been a great driver and before long, she'd taken over most of the driving, as Charlotte had never really enjoyed it. Driving was just a necessity to her; a means of getting from point A to point B. But Heather loved it.

The damned phone went off again. She looked at it. Him again. In frustration, she pressed the green dot. "What the hell do you want?!" she screamed into the phone.

There was silence for a moment. Then his voice. It still chilled her. "I just wanted to know why you didn't come to the funeral. Carla would be so disappointed. Her sister asked me why you weren't there. She thought maybe you were ill. Are you ill, Charlie?"

"I'm not going to discuss my personal business with you. Quit calling me."

"Now, Charlie. Is that any way to treat your best friend's grieving widower? Don't you want to comfort me?" he chuckled.

Charlotte ended the call. "Bastard!" she whispered.

She got up and went into her bedroom. She walked over to the desk and pulled out the letter. With shaking hands, she took the letter from the envelope and opened it to read it once again. The handwriting was difficult to read; apparently, the writer's hands had been quite shaky.

Dearest Charlie,

This is the most difficult letter I've ever had to write. But I must do it now, or it will never be written, I fear. I'm not doing well and haven't much time left. One of the few things that brings me comfort is remembering our years together as girls. Didn't we have a joyful childhood, Charlie? Climbing trees, playing baseball...we were such tomboys, you and me.

But I ruined everything later. Oh, I know we continued to have our little vacations over the years, meeting for a few days in places like New York, San Francisco, even that one time in Costa Rica. I loved the times we got together. But the truth is, I was not a good friend to you.

I need to apologize to you now, before it's too late. You see, I knew, Charlie. All this time, I knew what he did to you that night, so many years ago. And I did nothing about it. I tried to forget about it. I was weak. I thought I needed him. If it makes you feel any better, I'll tell you now that I paid for my sin. Paid for keeping his secret. All these years, I pretended to have this wonderful marriage with him. But he was a brute at times, Charlie. I'm not complaining, I know I deserved it. I doubt you'll take any comfort in knowing I was punished for my sin, because you're a much better person than I am.

I am also writing to Debra. You should hear from her; if not, please call her.

I'm so sorry, Charlie. You deserved so much better from your "best friend."
I love you like a sister. I'm sorry if my keeping his secret harmed you. What am I
saying? Of course, it did. I'm so, so sorry, sweet friend. I know you don't believe in
an afterlife, but if there is one, I hope I'll see you again someday.
Love, Carla

With trembling hands, Charlotte returned the letter to its envelope and placed it back in the desk drawer. She hadn't heard a word from Carla's daughter, Debra, and wondered if she would. Poor Carla. Charlotte hadn't even had time to reach out to her, for Carla was dead before she'd even received the letter. That monster had called her to tell her Carla was dead. She'd hung up on him but had later found the obituary online. Then the next day, she'd received the letter. That was when she decided to go on that tour bus to the casino. She'd known there was no way she could go to the funeral and face him. She'd been so angry. At him. And yes, at Carla. Not just for keeping the bastard's secret and never letting her know that she knew, but angry that Carla had stayed with him. Had put up with his sick, cruel behavior. She'd deserved better. Why hadn't Carla realized that?

And now, she kept getting these calls from him. Why the hell was he doing this to her after all this time? He was sick. Twisted. Maybe I should just change my phone number, she thought. I wonder if he has any idea that I've moved. He probably still has my old address. If I change the phone number, he won't be able to call me. I can change my e-mail address, too. My web site has no personal information about me. So, I should be safe. Right?

Charlotte sighed. After all these years, he still had power over her. After all, he's the reason she'd started drinking again. I'm pathetic, she thought. I've let him do this to me. What the hell is wrong with me? Maybe I should start going to meetings again. They helped years ago. But that was back when she still believed in a "higher power." Would she still find the meetings helpful? She doubted it.

She got up and made her way back to the living room. Lexi and Jade should be here in a few minutes. Where's my handbag? She walked around her apartment and found the handbag on the small table she had in the hall by the kitchen. Just as she reached for it, the doorbell rang. She walked to the front door, looked out the peephole and saw the two girls. She opened the door and Lexi smiled at her.

"Hello, Lexi. And you must be Jade."

The little girl smiled. "Hi."

"Well, come on in. Lexi will show you around the apartment before we leave. Do you have a phone?"

"No, ma'am."

"Well, I don't have a house phone so I'll leave my cell phone here on the coffee table so you can call out if you have any kind of emergency."

"Emergency?"

Charlotte smiled. "Well, I know I'm just being an old worrywart, I'm sure you'll be fine. But I'll feel better knowing you have the phone here."

"What do I do if someone calls you while you're gone?"

"Just ignore it. Whoever it is will leave a message or call back."

"Yes, ma'am."

Lexi gave Jade a quick tour, showing her where the hall bathroom and kitchen were.

"Jade, I think there are some cookies in the jar on the counter. Other than that, there isn't a whole lot to snack on. A few water bottles in the fridge. I'll have your sister take me by Randall's, so next time you come, there will be some snacks for you."

"Oh, that's okay. I don't need anything. Can I watch TV?"

"Sure."

Charlotte picked up the remote and handed it to Jade. "Do you know how to use this?"

Jade looked at it. "I think so." She turned on the TV, found the channel she wanted, and started watching.

Lexi spoke up. "Okay. We shouldn't be more than an hour. Don't answer the door to anyone, okay? And don't touch anything."

"I won't."

Lexi and Charlotte made their way out of the apartment and to the elevator. Lexi turned to Charlotte. "You don't need to bring your walker?"

"No, I don't think so."

"Do you need me to help you?"

"I'm fine, thank you."

They rode the elevator down to the first floor, and walked out of the building. She turned to the valet and gave him her car keys. As they waited, Lexi turned to Charlotte. "This is cool, having someone to go get your car for you."

"Yes, it is nice. On the other hand, it's also a good way for the management here to keep track of my comings and goings. Then report them to my son."

Lexi raised her eyebrows and appeared shocked. "They do that?!"

"Oh, I don't know. But I wouldn't put it past these tyrants."

The car pulled up and the valet opened the passenger door. Charlotte settled into the passenger seat as Lexi walked around the car and got in on the driver's side. She looked over at Charlotte. "I'm a little nervous. What do you want me to do now?"

"First, put your seat belt on. Then adjust your mirrors." She showed Lexi how to adjust the side mirrors. "Don't worry about being in a hurry. Just take your time. Now look around and if everything's clear, pull out and let's go find a place to park in the lot, while I go over some things with you and you can get used to the car."

Lexi nodded, put the car in drive, and slowly pulled away and headed to the parking lot. She parked in a space far from the building, with no other cars around it.

"You did great. Now, before I forget, I wanted to ask you, do you have one of those little manuals put out by the DMV with all of the driving rules?"

"Yes, ma'am. It's at home. But I use the online version."

"Can I borrow the manual then? The truth is, when you've been driving as long as I have, you just kind of do things without thinking. I want to be sure I'm giving you accurate information."

"Yes, ma'am, I'll bring it."

"Good. Okay, let me go over everything about the car with you, first. This is a hybrid, so it's a little different than a traditional gas guzzler."

Charlotte reviewed everything with Lexi, who listened patiently. "Now, why don't you just drive around the parking lot for a few minutes, practice parking, backing up, and so on? Then we'll head over to Randall's. It's only a couple of miles from here, and we'll take some side streets so you shouldn't get into any heavy traffic this first trip."

"Okay. That sounds good."

Lexi did as Charlotte asked and soon seemed to relax and feel a little more comfortable with her driving. She parked the car again and turned to Charlotte. "Do you think I'm ready to hit the road now?"

"Yes. You're doing fine. Oh, wait, where's your permit?"

"In my back pocket."

"Okay. The proof of insurance is in the glove box." Charlotte pulled it out and showed it to Lexi. "So, if you get stopped by a police officer, you'll know where it is."

"Stopped? Why would I be stopped?"

"Oh, I doubt you will be. But sooner or later, it happens to everyone. You might forget to turn on your signal when making a lane change, or drive a little too fast, nobody's perfect."

"Oh. God, I hope that doesn't happen today. That would be scary."

Charlotte pondered that statement. "Lexi, do you know how to react if you are stopped?"

"Well, I guess I'd pull over to the side of the road and roll down the window and see what the cop has to say."

Charlotte nodded. "I hate to bring this up, but you need to be extra careful. Keep your hands on the wheel so he can see them. Wait until he gives you instructions before reaching for your license or insurance card. Be very polite."

Lexi squinted at her. "Why do I need to be extra careful?"

Charlotte sighed. "You are Hispanic, right?"

"Yes."

"Well, I wish it wasn't so, but you never know when you might come across a racist cop. Lexi, I believe most police officers are good people with good intentions. But, as in any occupation, there are going to be some bad apples in the bunch, and when that is the case with police – well, the results can be devastating. I'm sure you're well aware of this issue. Have your parents not had discussions like this with you?"

Lexi looked surprised. "I can't believe you would even think about that."

"Because I'm an old white lady?"

"Well…no, I didn't mean that. You're not old."

"It's okay, Lexi. I am old."

"It's just, well, what would you know about something like that?"

"Personally? Absolutely nothing. In fact, your parents are probably the ones who should be discussing this with you. As you say, what would I know about it? Only what I've read."

Lexi scoffed. "Well, my mom is as white as you. Believe me, she has more to worry about from cops than the color of her skin."

Charlotte didn't pursue that statement about Lexi's mom. "And your dad?"

Lexi looked at her. "No longer in the picture."

Charlotte nodded. "Oh. Well, just be careful, okay? Let's hope you don't get stopped by a cop, anyway, at least not today."

"Okay."

Charlotte gave her instructions and they made their way to the grocery story. Lexi did fine, though she was extra cautious, as most beginning drivers are. Once she parked the car, she let out a big sigh as if she'd been holding her breath the entire time, and looked over at Charlotte. "Well, we made it."

"You did great, Lexi. You're a natural!"

Lexi looked pleased at the compliment. "You think so?"

"Oh, yes. You did much better than my children did when they first started driving. Or maybe I'm just more patient now." Charlotte chuckled. Wow, she thought to herself, is that really me, laughing?

They got out of the car and made their way into the grocery store. Lexi insisted she use one of the motorized grocery carts for disabled people. She felt a little foolish at first but she had to admit it was probably a good idea. With Lexi's assistance, she filled her cart with the items on her list. After Charlotte paid for the groceries, Lexi transferred the grocery bags to a regular cart and they left the motorized cart in the store. Charlotte pushed the cart, as it gave her something to hold onto, and Lexi walked along beside her. After loading the groceries, Lexi helped Charlotte get into the car. When it was time to back out of the parking space, Lexi turned to Charlotte.

"I'm a little nervous about backing up."

"Yes, that's a bit intimidating at first. Put your arm across the back of my seat and look out the rear window. Before pulling out, though, you can glance at the screen here; once you're in reverse, the backup camera will activate and you can also see what's behind you on the screen."

"Oh, that's so cool!"

"It is, isn't it? Also, I'll help you look, so don't be nervous. Okay, good, now that you have it in reverse and we both see it's clear, go ahead and back out slowly."

Lexi backed out without any problems. "Now, put it back in drive."

Ten minutes later, Lexi was pulling into the driveway in front of the retirement community.

"Do you still want to use the valet parking?"

"Yes. There's also a cart in the lobby which we can use to carry the groceries to my apartment."

As they rode up to Charlotte's apartment on the elevator, Lexi turned to her. "It was really nice of you to take me driving today, Ms. Tilian. And letting Jade stay in your apartment, too. Thank you."

"You're welcome. I enjoyed it."

When they entered the apartment, Jade was sitting just where they'd left her, but the TV was off and she was reading a book. She looked up at they walked in. "How'd you do, Lexi?"

"Okay. I didn't wreck the car, or anything."

"She did great!" said Charlotte.

Jade smiled. "Good! Was it fun?"

Lexi shrugged. "I don't know. Kind of. But I was a little nervous."

"Maybe you won't be so nervous next time, Lexi."

"Probably not. Jade, help me put these groceries away, okay?"

"Oh, you girls don't need to do that. I can take care of it."

"After what you did for us? No way, it's the least we can do."

Jade stood up and returned the book she'd been reading to Charlotte's bookcase. The girls carried the bags into the kitchen and started putting the groceries away. When they were finished, Lexi asked Jade, "Well, you ready to go?"

"Okay."

Charlotte spoke up. "When do you want to have another lesson?"

"I can't tomorrow, because I work too late on Tuesdays. I'm off Wednesday. How about Thursday, at five-thirty again? Will that work?"

"Absolutely." She turned to Jade. "So, do you stay home on Tuesdays, since Lexi works late?"

Before she could answer, Lexi spoke up. "She goes to our aunt's house on Tuesdays and plays with our cousins."

"Well, that's nice. So, your mom works evenings?"

"Uh, her schedule varies a lot."

"Oh. What does she do?"

"This and that. Well, we'd better hurry. We've got a couple blocks to walk. We're riding the bus home tonight."

"Oh. I'm sorry to keep you, then. Jade, if you like, you can borrow the book you were reading. I don't mind if you take it with you."

"That's okay. I'll just read it when we come back on Thursday."

"Okay. Well, you girls be careful going home."

"We will be," said Lexi. "Goodnight."

"Goodnight."

Charlotte locked the door behind them, then made her way to the back of the apartment. It was almost dusk. She opened the French doors and sat down at the table on her balcony. A few minutes later, she saw the girls cross the street and walk down the sidewalk, along the front of the park. She watched them walk the two blocks to the corner where the bus stop was and continued watching them until the bus pulled up and they stepped onto it. Only after the bus pulled away did she go back inside. She closed the doors and went into the kitchen. She took a frozen dinner out of the freezer, removed it from the box and popped it into the microwave. While it was heating, she opened the bottle of wine she'd bought, and filled a wine glass. A few minutes later, she was sitting at the kitchen table, enjoying her dinner and listening to some nice music on the local jazz station. She smiled to herself. This had been a good day.

Chapter 10

Over the next couple of weeks, Charlotte and the girls settled into a routine. Charlotte had her physical therapy on Monday and Thursday mornings. Every Monday, Thursday and Friday, Charlotte and Lexi had a driving lesson. The first Tuesday was a long, boring day for Charlotte. The second week, she convinced Lexi to let Jade spend Tuesday evening with her. They had a fun evening, baking cupcakes and watching a movie. She and Jade planned what they would do the next Tuesday. There was no talk of going to an aunt's house to play with cousins, and Charlotte suspected there was no aunt, no cousins. Wednesdays were the worst day of the week for Charlotte. The girls didn't come to the retirement community and she had to find ways to fill the day on her own.

On the second Saturday after the driving lessons had started, all three of Charlotte's children called to wish her happy birthday. Heather sent balloons, Julie sent chocolate covered strawberries, and John sent flowers. That evening, the activities director called and asked her to come to the lobby. She knew something was up, but being in a good mood after speaking with her children, she decided to go along and rode the elevator down to the first floor. When she entered the lobby, a group of residents, most of whom she had never met, cheered "Happy Birthday!" and blew party horns. There was cake and ice cream and punch. In spite of herself, Charlotte was touched that these people had taken time to help her celebrate her birthday. She didn't want to admit it, but this was a little better than sitting by herself in her apartment on her seventieth birthday.

The best part of the two-week period, though, was that the unwanted phone calls had stopped. At first, she kept picking up her phone to check if she had missed a call, but there was nothing. She began to relax and hoped that he had finally decided to quit torturing her. She started sleeping better and the bottle of wine she'd bought during that first driving lesson was still half full. On the other hand, she'd also heard nothing from Debra. Maybe she should call her but frankly, it was nice to just put the whole thing behind her.

Sunday morning, Charlotte slept in, then enjoyed the newspaper and a cup of coffee on the balcony. It started to get pretty hot outside, though, so she soon moved back into the air-conditioned apartment. As she closed the French doors, the front doorbell rang. Who on earth could that be? She looked out the peephole and saw Lexi and Jade standing on her doorstop. What on earth? She opened the door and the girls smiled and held out a gift bag with a big red bow on it. "Happy Birthday, Ms. Tilian!" they both exclaimed.

Charlotte smiled and shook her head. "You girls! What a nice surprise. But you shouldn't have done this, you didn't need to get me anything."

Lexi said, "Oh, okay. Well, bye then." She turned as if to walk away and Jade looked shocked.

"Lexi!"

Lexi turned back around and laughed. "Just kidding!"

Charlotte laughed and let them in. "Don't you girls have anything better to do on a Sunday than spend it with a grouchy old woman like me?"

"Not really," replied Jade. "Besides, you aren't grouchy, you're nice."

Charlotte looked at Jade. "There are a lot of people who would disagree with you."

"Well, they'd be wrong. Now open your present - please!"

They sat down in the living room and Charlotte reached in the bag. There was a cute handmade card which she suspected Jade had made. On the front, was a drawing of two girls, one slightly taller than the other, and a grey-haired woman. She looked at the girls. "These people look familiar."

Lexi smiled and Jade giggled. On the inside of the card was a message: "Happy Birthday, Ms. Tilian, our favorite author and best friend." Jade and Lexi had both signed the card and added some X's and O's. Charlotte felt a lump in her throat.

"I think since we're best friends now, we should drop the Ms. Tilian nonsense. My name is Charlotte. Okay?"

The girls looked at each other. They smiled and nodded.

"Good. Now, what else is in this bag?"

She pulled out a paperback of a novel written by one of her favorite authors, Catherine Ryan Hyde.

"Oh, this is wonderful! I haven't read this one yet. Is it her latest?"

The girls looked so pleased with themselves. "Yes, ma'am," said Lexi. "I hope you don't mind that it's a paperback."

"Not at all. In fact, with my weak left hand, it's easier to read a lighter book. This is a perfect gift. Thank you both so much. I love it and can't wait to read it."

The girls were beaming.

"Now, how about some cake? I have some left over from yesterday."

Later, as they were eating the cake, Lexi spoke up. "I'm sorry we couldn't be here yesterday, Charlotte."

"Oh, don't worry about that. I was surprised that I didn't see you, though. Don't you usually work on Saturdays?"

"Yes, usually. But I had to help my mom with some stuff yesterday."

"Is she alright?"

Lexi's fork paused midway from her plate to her mouth. She considered the question. "She'll live."

Lexi continued eating cake. Charlotte looked over at Jade, who seemed to be avoiding Charlotte's gaze.

"This cake is really good, Charlotte," said Jade.

Charlotte decided not to question the girls any further about their mother or what they were doing yesterday. "It is, isn't it? Would you like another piece?"

"Oh, no, ma'am. Thank you, but this is plenty."

"Lexi, more cake?"

"No, thanks, Charlotte. Actually, Jade and I probably should go."

"Oh, okay. Would you like to take some cake home?"

"Are you sure you have enough? It's your birthday cake, you should enjoy it."

"Oh, I have more than I need. I'd just end up throwing it away. Let me box some up for you."

"That would be great. Thanks."

Soon the girls were gone and once again, the apartment was quiet.

Charlotte made her way to the balcony and watched the girls walk up the street. This time, Jade looked back over her shoulder, saw Charlotte, and nudged Lexi to get her attention. She said something to Lexi, who then looked up and also saw Charlotte. Both girls waved and Charlotte waved back. Again, she waited until the bus came and as the girls stepped on the bus, they looked back and waved goodbye at Charlotte. As the bus pulled away, Charlotte sighed and turned to go back inside. Her cell phone began to ring.

Chapter 11

She looked at the number. The 505 area code was unfamiliar to her. She answered. "Hello?"

A woman's voice asked, "Hello. Is this Charlotte Tilian?"

"Who's calling?"

"My name is Debra. I believe you and my mother, Carla, were friends?"

Charlotte sat down. "Yes. Yes, that's right. I'm Charlotte."

"Oh, good. I've been trying to reach you, but apparently, I had the wrong number."

"Oh. Your mother said you'd be calling me, and I wondered why I hadn't heard from you."

"Yes, well, I had to do a little detective work to find your number."

"Oh? So, how did you find it?"

"Well, my dad's visiting. I didn't want to tell him I was trying to reach you. So, while he was showering last night, I snuck a peek at his cell phone. You were in his contacts list."

Charlotte felt her heart beating faster. "I was? Am?"

"Yes, ma'am."

"Just my phone number? Or my address, too?"

"There's an address. Houston, right?"

"What street?"

"Street? Let's see, I made a note of it...Clay. Is that right?"

Charlotte felt relief flood over her. He still had her old address. She replied, "Yes, that's right. So, where is your father now?"

"He's out playing golf."

"Debra, where do you live? Are you still in California?"

"No ma'am, we're in Santa Fe now. We moved here last year. My husband was transferred here with his job."

"Oh, Santa Fe is lovely."

"It is, isn't it? Have you spent much time here?"

"I used to travel to Santa Fe quite a bit. I took some writing courses there. Something about the place just spurs creativity."

Debra laughed. "It does do that. I've even taken a couple of art classes. I'm not very good, but it's fun."

"Did Carla have a chance to visit you in Santa Fe?"

"Just once, right after we moved here. She got sick soon after that and wasn't able to travel."

"Debra, I was so sad to hear about Carla. I'm sure you must miss her so much."

"Yes. I do. But, Charlotte, you and I really need to talk. My dad is leaving tomorrow. Is there any way we could meet in person? If I need to, I can make a trip to Houston."

"Oh. Well. I don't know." Charlotte was apprehensive. She hadn't spoken to Debra since she was a child. Could she trust her? What if she was in cahoots with her father?

She asked Debra, "Why is it so important to meet in person? Can't you say what you need to say over the phone?"

"I could. But I'd feel better meeting with you in person. Look, I know there's some reason you want to avoid my dad. Frankly, I wish I could avoid him, too. I do, as much as possible. He treated my mother horribly. But you know how it is – he's my dad. Though we aren't close, I try to maintain a civil relationship with him. I know Mom wanted me to meet with you, and that she didn't want him to know anything about it. In fact, it's imperative he knows nothing about it. I understand you don't really know me, but you can trust me. Didn't Mom send you a letter, telling you I'd be contacting you? Because she wrote to me and said she was writing you, also."

"Yes. She did."

"You trusted Mom, right? So, don't you think you can trust me, too? She wouldn't have wanted you and I to meet, otherwise. Right?"

Charlotte thought how she had trusted Carla, but then learned she'd kept quiet all those years about what had happened. However, she just said to Debra, "I suppose you're right."

"So, may I visit you? It will probably be a week or two before I can come that way."

Charlotte considered it. "Let me think about it, Debra. I've had some medical issues, myself." She hated to use the stroke as an excuse, but figured it would buy her a little time to think about Debra visiting.

"Oh, I'm sorry. Are you okay?"

"I will be. I'll call you back in a couple of days, okay? You said he's leaving tomorrow?"

"Yes. His flight leaves early tomorrow morning. He's going back to Philadelphia."

"Okay. Well, you'll hear from me no later than Wednesday."

"Okay, thank you."

"Goodbye, Debra."

"Goodbye, Charlotte."

Chapter 12

Monday afternoon, Lexi and Jade showed up at 5:40. Charlotte had prepared a snack for Jade and when she and Lexi left the apartment, Jade was happily munching on some crackers and cheese and reading the book which she and Lexi had given Charlotte for her birthday. Charlotte had finished the book in two days and had thoroughly enjoyed it. As Lexi pulled out of the driveway and turned onto the street, Charlotte asked her how far away her high school was.

"Oh, I don't know. Not too far. Probably fifteen minutes or so."

Charlotte smiled. People nowadays rarely answered in miles when asked how far away something was, it was always how much time it took to get there. Probably because traffic was so terrible in Houston.

"Well, let's drive there. I'd like to see where you go to school."

"Oh, well, okay but I don't go there anymore."

"Why not?"

"I'm finished. Got my diploma. Jade still has another week and a half of school, but I'm done forever."

"You graduated?"

"Yes, ma'am."

"Oh, my. I'm so sorry I missed that. I would've loved to have seen that."

"Nothing to see."

Charlotte thought a moment. "You didn't go to the commencement?"

"Nope."

"Why on earth not?"

Lexi shrugged. "Didn't see any point in it. I got my diploma, that's all I need."

"Did you at least celebrate with your friends? Or your family?"

Lexi glanced over at her then back at the road.

"Not really."

"So, what about college?"

"What about it?"

"Where do you plan to attend? And what do you plan to study?"

"Plan?" Lexi laughed. "I have no plans, Charlotte. Other than trying to find a better paying job."

"Oh, no! You must go to college. A young woman as intelligent as you are! Lexi, what are you thinking?! Not go to college?!"

"Charlotte, no offense, but you and I don't live in the same world. I'm sure going to college was a given for you – and your kids – but in my world, it just isn't possible."

"Well, the truth is, I didn't start college until I was forty-five years old. I celebrated my fiftieth birthday and my college graduation the same year. But I wouldn't recommend that; starting right out of high school would have been a better option, believe me."

"You were forty-five when you started college? What was the point?"

Charlotte laughed. "The point was to improve my life."

"Did you?"

"I certainly did. I turned my whole life around. And that's when I started writing."

"Wait a minute. You didn't start writing books until you were in your forties?"

"Actually, I wrote short stories and poetry for a few years. And I think I was fifty-two when my first novel was published."

"Wow. So, I guess it's never too late, huh?"

"That's true. But, Lexi, don't wait as long as I did. Isn't there something you'd like to study? What do you want to do?"

"You mean what do I wanna be when I grow up?"

Charlotte smiled. "Something like that. Yes."

Lexi shrugged. "I don't really think about it. I mean, I have to work. And then there's Jade."

"Jade?"

But Lexi turned into a parking lot and announced, "This is it, Charlotte. My high school."

She pulled into an empty parking space and they sat and looked at the school. There weren't many people around at this time of day but a woman carrying a messenger bag was walking down a sidewalk from the school to the parking lot.

"Oh, look. There's Mrs. Lewis, my English teacher." She turned to Charlotte. "Would you mind if I introduced you to her? She'd probably get a kick out of meeting you, being an English teacher and all."

Charlotte shrugged. "Sure. Let's talk to Mrs. Lewis."

They both got out of the car and Lexi called out to her teacher, who smiled as soon as she recognized Lexi. She walked over to the two of them and exclaimed, "Why, Lexi Hernandez! It's so good to see you! How are you?"

Lexi smiled back at her. "I'm fine, Mrs. Lewis. I was just showing my friend where I went to school. Mrs. Lewis, I'd like you to meet Charlotte Tilian. Charlotte, this is Mrs. Lewis, my senior English teacher."

Mrs. Lewis looked surprised and shook Charlotte's hand. "It's Helen. Not *the* Charlotte Tilian, famous author and poet?"

"Yes!" answered Lexi.

"I'm pleased to meet you, Helen."

"Oh, the pleasure is mine. Lexi, why didn't you tell me that you and Charlotte Tilian were friends? This is amazing. I just love your poetry, Ms. Tilian. Lexi, you've been keeping your friend a secret!"

"Well, we're new friends. We haven't known each other long, have we Charlotte?"

"No, but we've become fast friends. Helen, I'm sure Lexi was one of your best students, right?"

"Not one of the best – *the* best. I look forward to hearing great things about you, Lexi."

Lexi smiled. "Thanks, Mrs. Lewis."

Charlotte spoke up. "Lexi and I were just discussing college. I'm trying to convince her that a young woman of her obvious intelligence needs to continue her education."

"Oh, absolutely! Lexi, have you not applied anywhere?"

"Not yet, no."

"Well, you need to. If finances are an issue, you know there are all kinds of scholarships and loans available. Didn't you meet with Mr. Hector, the guidance counselor?"

"No, ma'am. I mean, I did go see him once, but he didn't have a whole lot of information that helped me. I didn't bother to apply because I know how expensive it is. And Mr. Hector thought trade school would be best for me. He mentioned cosmetology school, but I'm not interested in that, I can barely manage to fix my own hair. But it's okay. I'll get a good job and save my money, then go to college later, like Charlotte did."

Mrs. Lewis shook her head. "Lexi, I want you to come see me and we'll get you into a college this fall. I know there are options out there for you but you need to hurry; you should've started this process months ago. Can you come by Wednesday around one o'clock? I don't have any afternoon classes now that you seniors have graduated. Which reminds me – I didn't see you at graduation the other night."

"Yes, ma'am, I know." She looked down. "I guess I could come by on Wednesday, but really, you don't need to worry about me. I'll figure it out."

"I'm sure you will. But I want to help. I have a lot of experience at helping my students navigate their way through college and scholarship applications. I know I can help you."

Lexi shrugged. "Well, okay. I'll see you Wednesday. Thanks."

"Great! I'll see you then. Ms. Tilian, it was so nice to meet you." She turned and walked away and Charlotte and Lexi got back in the Prius.

"Well, she seems nice," said Charlotte.

"Yeah. She is." Lexi seemed deep in thought and Charlotte kept quiet. The poor girl seemed to have a lot on her mind.

55

As they rode the elevator up to her apartment, Charlotte asked Lexi, "So, how will you get to the school Wednesday afternoon?"

"I'll ride my bike."

"What does Jade do on Wednesdays?"

"She's still in school, remember?"

"Oh, that's right."

They entered Charlotte's apartment and Lexi helped Jade gather her belongings. "Did you do your homework, Jade?" Lexi inquired.

"Yes. I just had a few math problems. It's in my backpack if you want to check it later."

"Okay. Well, let's go."

"Girls?"

They both turned to her. "Yes?" asked Lexi.

"On Thursday, bring your best outfits to change into after school and work. I'd like you to accompany me somewhere and you need to dress nicely."

"Where?" asked Jade, excitedly.

"It's a surprise. I think you'll like it. And be sure your mom is okay with your getting home a little late – probably around nine, if that isn't too late for you on a school night, Jade. She can call me if she wants, and I'll let her know the plans. And I'll make sure you get home safely."

Lexi looked skeptical. "Do we have to wear dresses?"

"No. Just something nice. You can wear dresses if you want to, but it's not necessary."

"So, no driving lesson?"

"No, not on Thursday."

"How will we get where we're going?"

Charlotte smiled again. "That's part of the surprise."

Jade jumped up and down and clapped her hands. "Oh, boy! I love surprises!" She hugged Charlotte around the waist. "You're the greatest, Ms. T!"

Charlotte was surprised by the show of affection but hugged Jade and said, "No, you're the greatest!"

"So, you want us here at the usual time? After school for Jade, five-thirty for me?"

Charlotte nodded.

"Okay."

As the girls left, Lexi turned back, "Thank you for the driving lesson today, Charlotte."

"And for the snack," said Jade.

Charlotte waved them off. "Go on, you two. I'll see you tomorrow. Jade, you're spending the afternoon with me, right?"

Lexi spoke up. "We won't be here tomorrow, Charlotte. They changed my schedule and now I'm off Tuesdays and Wednesdays. Since I'm done with school now, I'm going to be working various hours, but usually nine to five-thirty, every day except Tuesday, Wednesday and Sunday. So, I guess I'll have to cut back on the driving lessons."

"You could come up here on your days off, if you like."

"Wish I could, but I've got some other stuff to do."

"Oh. Well, okay. Just know the offer stands. This is my final week of PT, so starting next week, my schedule is free and clear."

"Thank you, Charlotte. Well, we'd better go. We're riding the bus today and if we miss it, we'll have to wait another hour before the next one."

"Oh, well, hurry along then. Bye, girls."

"Bye. We'll watch for you on the balcony," said Jade.

Charlotte nodded and closed the door behind them. She made her way to the balcony and sat down. Soon, she saw the girls walking down the sidewalk. Jade looked up and waved and kept chattering away to Lexi about something. Charlotte smiled. She remained on the balcony and watched the girls as they waited on the bench at the bus stop. Out of the corner of her eye, she noticed a black pickup pull into the parking lot across the street. The driver got out and stood by the truck, looking around the park as if trying to find someone.

Charlotte realized it was the same man she'd seen that day, standing over Jade in the park until he was hit by the soccer ball. "Don't look at the bus stop, don't look at the bus stop," Charlotte muttered to herself. But he looked at the bus stop. The girls were busy talking and seemed oblivious to their surroundings. Charlotte sensed this man was a danger to them. She started waving, trying to get their attention but they didn't notice her. The man was now halfway to the bus stop. She stood. Just then the bus drove up, the girls stood, and as they stepped on the bus, they turned and started to wave at Charlotte but they saw the man and hurried on the bus. The man started to run toward the bus and was waving, as if to try and get the bus driver to stop, but thankfully, the bus pulled away from the curb and the man was left standing on the sidewalk.

Charlotte had her hand on her chest. "Thank God! They're safe," she thought.

Then the man turned and looked up as if to try and figure out who the girls had been waving to; his eyes locked with Charlotte's. She felt a cold chill. Finally, he looked away from her and walked back toward his truck. She sat down and watched him. As he opened the door to his truck, the man looked back up at her and raised his hand in a quick wave. She didn't acknowledge him. He climbed in the truck and pulled out of the parking lot.

Chapter 13

Over the next two days, Charlotte was a nervous wreck. How she wished she had a way to contact Lexi! But later on Wednesday afternoon, she remembered – Lexi was going to spend the afternoon with Helen Lewis, the English teacher. Maybe she could reach her. She looked up the number to Lexi's high school and called and asked if she could speak with Helen Lewis. The woman who answered the phone told Charlotte she'd have a student aide go to Mrs. Lewis' classroom with a message to call her.

"That's fine. But can the student please tell Mrs. Lewis it's somewhat of an emergency? Tell her Charlotte is calling and I'm worried about a mutual friend. Here's my number." Charlotte gave the number and disconnected. About five minutes later, her phone rang.

"Hello?"

"Is this Charlotte?"

"Yes. Helen?"

"Yes. My goodness, has something happened to Lexi? Danny said there was an emergency."

"She's not with you?"

"She left about twenty minutes ago. I offered to drive her home but she said she had her bike and was fine. What's happened?"

Charlotte sighed with relief. "Oh, I'm so glad to hear she's alright. I've been worrying about her and Jade so much, after something I saw yesterday. But she seemed okay today while she was with you?"

Helen laughed. "Well, you know Lexi. Always seems a little on edge, never completely relaxed. But I didn't notice anything out of the ordinary today, nothing that concerned me. In fact, she seemed pretty happy when she left. I think I've convinced her to try and attend school, at least part-time, in the fall. But you said you saw something. Can you tell me about it?"

Charlotte explained about the man she'd seen twice now, and her fears that he might harm the girls. Helen told Charlotte, "You know, so many of the children I've taught over the years live in situations that would horrify you. There's no telling what kind of situation Lexi and her sister are dealing with at home. She's pretty tight-lipped about it. I've never met her parents and I'm not sure what her family life is like, but I can guess based on what I've observed and things she has said."

"Such as?"

"Well, for starters, that tough shell she has which is impossible to crack. I'd be willing to bet my salary that if you were to ask her about the man with the black pickup, she'd act as if she didn't have a clue who you're talking about. There's also the fact that she's such a good student, yet nobody from her family has ever stepped foot in this school for special events that involved Lexi, like open house, parent-teacher night, and so on. She didn't participate in extracurricular activities, didn't seem to have any close friends. Like most of the children here, she lives in a very impoverished area. Then there was the incident surrounding her arm."

"What incident?"

"A few months ago, Lexi missed three days of school in a row. When she came back to school, she was wearing a sling on her left arm and she was more withdrawn than ever. After class, I stopped her as she was walking out, and tried to ask her about it. But she was very vague. Her excuses reminded me of things you hear battered women say."

"What do you mean?"

"Oh, you know…minimizing the injury, she was just clumsy, it was nothing to worry about, she was fine."

"But you didn't believe her."

"No. I even mentioned it to our school counselor but he didn't seem concerned at all."

"Mr. Hector?"

Charlotte heard Helen sigh. "Yes, Mr. Hector. I suppose I should be generous and say he's just overworked and trying to do an impossible job, but honestly, the man's incompetence infuriates me."

"So, you don't really know anything about Lexi's family?"

"No. I was hoping you might, since you're a friend."

Charlotte explained how she knew Lexi and Jade.

"Oh. Well, you wouldn't know either, then."

"No, but I'm taking the girls out to dinner tomorrow. I've asked Lexi to have her mother call me. And I plan on taking them home. So, I should have a better idea after that."

"Oh, I doubt it."

"Really? Why?"

"Let's see. Mom won't call you and Lexi will have a good explanation why. When you offer to take the girls home, they'll either have some other arrangements already or they'll jump out of the car so fast, you won't even have time to get out of the car and walk to their front door before they'll be inside with the door closed and locked behind them. And they'll probably tell you Mom is sick or is at work or something."

Charlotte nodded. "You're right. I need to be a step ahead of them and think through my plan a bit."

"Well, good luck. I'm glad Lexi and Jade have you as a friend. Between the two of us, maybe we can at least help Lexi get a good start in life after high school."

"I'm just glad that she made it to your appointment and seems to be okay."

"Me, too."

"Bye, Helen."

"Goodbye. I hope you'll keep in touch with me about Lexi."

"I will. Thanks."

They ended the call and Charlotte sat back in her chair, thinking over their conversation. Then her phone alerted her to another call. She glanced at the number. Damn! Him again.

Chapter 14

Charlotte ignored the call. She went into the kitchen and poured herself a tall glass of wine. No sitting on the balcony today, it was way too hot outside. She returned to the living room and sat on the couch, sipping her wine and mulling over things. The phone rang again. This time, it appeared to be Debra calling. She hadn't called her back yet, regarding a visit. She set down the wine glass, picked up the phone, and answered.

"Hello, Charlotte. It's me, Debra, again."

"Hi, Debra, how are you?"

"I'm fine, thanks."

"I've been thinking about our visit, I promise. I'm sorry I haven't called you."

"That's okay. I think we have a bigger problem."

"What do you mean?"

"My dad."

"What about him?"

"I think he's in Houston. And I'm guessing that could be a problem."

Charlotte froze. In Houston? She looked over at the door. It was locked, but she got up and went to the door, turned the dead bolt and secured the chain. She felt ill.

"Charlotte? You still there?"

"Yes. Yes, of course." She sat back down. "What makes you think he's in Houston?"

"Well, he called me a couple of hours ago. Said his flight had had an emergency landing in Houston and he may have to stay overnight. I've learned over the years not to trust anything he tells me. So, I go online to see if I can find anything about an emergency landing in Houston. Nothing. That seemed odd, but I wasn't overly concerned. Then, I decided to straighten up the guest room, where he'd stayed while he was here. You know, change the sheets, empty the trash, dust."

"Yes."

"Well, I got extra snoopy and looked through the trash. I taped together a printout of his flight itinerary home. Charlotte, he didn't have a flight reserved back to Philadelphia. The reservation was for Houston."

"No!"

"Uh huh. So, he's been in Houston over two hours. Did he say anything to you about coming to Houston?"

"No. But I don't talk with your dad, Debra."

"Yeah. I get that."

"Why would he come to Houston? Do you think it's to see me? If so, why?"

"Well, that's part of the reason why I wanted to meet with you. He may have discovered something my mom did."

"What's that?"

"She left you some money, Charlotte."

"She what?"

"She didn't want him to know about it. Years ago, she made some investments without his knowledge. She also had a life insurance policy he didn't know about, in which you and I are the beneficiaries. If he found out about that, he'd be pretty angry. I don't know how well you know my dad, but he can be really controlling, especially when it comes to money. He'd be livid if he knew about this. Maybe he found out somehow, and he wants to talk you out of the money. Or just bully you somehow, out of spite."

Charlotte nodded to herself, knowing Debra was right. He wouldn't be happy at all. But what would he be willing to do about it? He was an old man now. He had to be close to eighty. Was he still capable of violence?

"So, anyway, what do you think we should do?" asked Debra.

"Do?"

"Well, I mean, I thought about calling him and confronting him, but I don't know if that would make matters worse for you. Then I thought maybe I should rush to Houston and watch over you for a few days, make sure he doesn't harass you. Or maybe you could come here? I know you said you had some type of medical issue going on, though."

"Debra, tell me – is your father still in good health? Physically, is he still strong? I know he's got to be close to eighty now."

"Oh, he's strong as an ox. Still plays golf a few times a week, works out at the gym. He's seventy-nine but you'd never know it to look at him. He'll probably live to be at least a hundred. You know what they say – only the good die young."

That figures, thought Charlotte. "Well, I'm only seventy but I had a stroke recently and though I've recovered quite a bit, I'm not as strong as I once was. So, your father could present a threat to me if he wanted."

"Oh, surely he wouldn't do anything physical. But he can be very intimidating."

"Did he ever get physical with your mother? With you?"

She was met with silence. Finally, Debra answered. "You're right. You have every reason to feel threatened. Charlotte, do you live alone?"

"Not exactly. I mean, I'm in a safe place as long as I stay home."

"So, there are other people around who can protect you?"

"Yes."

"Good."

"Debra, you just stay tight. Stay in Santa Fe. I may figure out a way to visit you, if that would be alright."

"Absolutely! You can stay here at our house, or if you prefer, I can reserve a room for you at a local hotel. Whatever you prefer, just let me know."

"Okay. Let me see what I can do at this end, and I'll call you back."

"Okay. And Charlotte?"

"Yes?"

"Even without the money thing, I'm glad you're coming. Mom loved you so much and it will be good to spend time with you – it will be like having a connection to her, you know?"

"Yes, I do know. You take care, Debra. Thanks for calling me."

"You bet. Stay safe."

They ended the call.

Charlotte started thinking about what she should do, knowing he was in Houston. She got up and went to the desk in her bedroom. She sat down and started up the computer. She started searching for society news out of Philadelphia and found some photos that might be helpful. She printed out a couple of them, then shut down the computer. She grabbed the photos and her keys and made her way down to the lobby. At the receptionist's desk, she asked to speak with Peter, the head concierge.

"Ms. Tilian! What a pleasure! How can I assist you, dear?"

"Peter, have you seen this man in our building?" She shoved the photos toward him.

He seemed surprised by her question, but picked up the photos and looked at them. To his credit, he studied them carefully. "I don't believe so, Ms. Tilian. Is he a friend of yours?"

Charlotte shook her head emphatically. "No friend of mine, Peter. In fact, if he comes in here and asks for me, please send him away. Don't give him any information about me. Don't even confirm that I live here or that you know me. Do you understand?"

"Yes, of course. Ms. Tilian, has this man harmed you? Is this a police matter?"

"We don't need to involve the police, Peter. Just be sure he gets no further than this reception area, alright?"

"Yes, ma'am."

"Thank you, Peter."

"Ms. Tilian?"

"Yes?"

"Is your son aware of this – situation? Should we call him?"

"No!" she replied, a little too loudly, she suspected.

Peter just nodded. "Very well."

Charlotte pulled a twenty-dollar bill out of her pocket and handed it to Peter. "For your trouble, Peter."

"Oh, it's no trouble, Ms. Tilian. But thank you." He accepted the money and smiled at her. "If I see the gentleman in question, I will let you know."

"That would be good. Thanks again."

She turned and walked back to the elevator. She had a lot of planning to do.

Chapter 15

Charlotte spent the rest of the evening sitting at her computer, doing research, and making notes. After a couple of hours, she sat back and reviewed her notes. She had information on the DMV and taking a driver's test, stalking ordinances in Houston, powers of attorney, hotels in Santa Fe as well as places to stay between Houston and Santa Fe, local car rentals, and recent activities surrounding Carla's widower. What else? Let's see, what was Debra's last name? She searched her memory banks and finally it came to her. She googled the name but didn't find much and what she did find was not concerning in any way. Her husband was an administrator of a psychiatric hospital in Santa Fe, one of several in a nationwide organization. That explained the job transfer.

She sat back and stretched and yawned. She felt a bit hungry. She got up and as she did, noticed the walker leaning against the foot of her bed. She walked over to it, folded it, and placed it in her closet. She wouldn't be needing that anymore. Later, after dinner, she returned to the closet to figure out what to wear tomorrow night. She decided on an outfit, but what about shoes? She was still a little too shaky to wear any of the heels but she didn't want to wear ugly, "old lady shoes," either. She really needed a new pair of shoes; something dressy but safe. She called downstairs.

"Good evening, Ms. Tilian, how may I assist you?"

"Hello. Is it too late to make a reservation with the van tomorrow?"

"I don't believe so. Let me take a look at tomorrow's schedule. Well, there are a few rides booked already but perhaps around ten? Where do you need to go?"

"I'm not sure. I need to shop for a pair of shoes."

"Oh, well, if you can wait until eleven o'clock, there's a group going shopping then. I'm sure that would work."

"What time are they returning?"

"Let's see. They're also planning to be out for lunch, so Jerry is picking them up from the shopping center at two o'clock."

"Yes, that will work for me, then. Please add me to the list."

"Wonderful. Thank you, Ms. Tilian."

"Thank you."

Chapter 16

The next morning, her alarm clock woke her at seven. Lexi had told her she'd be by to clean the apartment at eight-thirty. She showered and dressed, made the bed, then went into the kitchen and started the coffee. She checked the fridge to be sure she still had plenty of vanilla flavored creamer – Lexi loved that in her coffee. She looked at the clock – still another forty-five minutes before Lexi's arrival. She thought about sitting outside with her morning coffee, but then remembered he was in Houston and decided against it. The last thing she needed was for him to spot her on the balcony. She realized she was being paranoid; after all, Houston is a huge city and as far as she knew, he still thought she lived in her Clay Street condo. That wasn't too far from here, though, and she didn't want to take any chances. She went into the living room and turned on the stereo. She picked up her e-reader and decided to order a new book to read. Soon, she was enjoying an unusual story about a woman in Cambridge, England who trained a gossamer hawk, during a time when she was also dealing with the grief of her father's death.

At eight-thirty, the doorbell buzzed. She got up and looked out the peephole to confirm it was Lexi, before opening the door.

"Hi, Charlotte. I've got mine and Jade's outfits for tonight." She held up a grocery bag. "I hope they'll be okay."

"I'm sure they'll be perfect. Why don't we hang them up in my closet, so they won't be all wrinkled?"

"Okay."

Lexi followed her into the bedroom and placed the bag on the bed. Charlotte went into the closet and brought out a few hangers. As Lexi pulled the clothes out of the bag, she looked up at Charlotte. "Are these clothes dressy enough?"

"Oh, yes. These are perfect!" Charlotte looked at the black jeans and blouses and made a mental note to herself that she should probably change her plans regarding her own outfit for tonight; she didn't want to be overdressed in comparison. She'd still need new shoes, though.

"I also brought sandals for us to wear; they're in my backpack. I figured sneakers probably wouldn't work, right?"

"Good thinking. Sandals will be great. In fact, that gives me an idea. I was thinking I might need new shoes, since I can't wear anything with much of a heel these days. But I'll bet I have a pair of sandals that will work." Charlotte went back into the walk-in closet and found a pair of flat sandals, with a rubberized sole. "Yep, these should work." She held them out for Lexi to see.

"Those are pretty, Ms. T. So, what are you going to wear?"

"Well, I have a pair of navy slacks. I think I'll wear them with a pretty tunic my daughter gave me for Mother's Day last year. Then dress it up a little with some jewelry."

Lexi nodded. "That sounds nice. Well, I'd better get started on the cleaning."

"Okay. Help yourself to coffee. There's creamer in the fridge."

"Thanks."

Charlotte hung the girls' clothes in the closet and found the pants and tunic she'd told Lexi about. Actually, the outfit would look quite nice with the sandals. She then found the cell phone and called downstairs to cancel her reservation on the van. She was relieved she wouldn't have to socialize with the rest of the van riders.

As Lexi cleaned the apartment, Charlotte continued reading her hawk book. Just before Lexi left, her cell phone rang again. The phone was on the kitchen table and Lexi picked it up to bring it to her.

"You know someone in Pennsylvania, Ms. T?" She handed the phone to Charlotte.

"No." She took the phone and looked at the number; it was him. "I had a friend who lived there but she passed away recently." She ignored the call. "How did you know the call was from Pennsylvania?"

"The area code. I have an uncle who lives there. He used to call my mom once in a while but he hasn't called in a long time. I don't know if he even lives there anymore."

"That's too bad. So, tell me about your family, Lexi. Any other uncles or aunts? Grandparents? You mentioned an aunt and cousins here in Houston once."

"I did?"

"I think so. Right after we met. You mentioned something about an aunt and cousins that Jade spent time with sometimes while you were at work."

Lexi blushed. "Oh, yeah. Well, we aren't very close. In fact, we really don't have much family. There's my mom, as you know. Oh, hey, that reminds me." She pulled a piece of paper from her pocket. "My mom wrote this to you. She doesn't have phone service right now, due to some mix-up with Verizon, so she wrote you this note."

Charlotte took the note from Lexi and read it. "Dear Ms. Tilian. Lexi and Jade told me you are taking them somewhere Thursday night as a surprise and you wanted to get my permission. It is okay with me. If there is any type of emergency, you can call my neighbors, Jimmy and Tamara. Lexi and Jade know their number. Thanks. Regina."

Charlotte looked over at Lexi, who was now dusting the bookshelves. "Well. I'm disappointed that I won't get to speak with your mother but I guess it can't be helped. Thank you for having her write the note." Lexi didn't look back at her but said, "No problem."

Charlotte folded up the note and lay it down on the coffee table. "So, Jimmy and Tamara. Are they good friends?"

Lexi turned back to her. "Neighbors. They're okay. I mean, it's not like we hang out with them, or anything. But Jimmy keeps an eye on things for us."

"An eye on things?"

"Oh, you know. Makes sure we're safe. Helps out if something breaks down, asks if we need anything if he's going to the store. He used to work in construction but he got laid off so now he just does odd jobs when he can. He can build anything, though. He made a table for Tamara for Christmas. It's beautiful. Just as nice as anything that guy Clint has made on Fixer Upper."

"Fixer Upper?"

"Yeah. You know, on HGTV?"

"I'm not familiar with it."

"You're kidding!"

Charlotte shrugged. "No."

Lexi picked up the remote and found HGTV. "Darn, it's a different show right now. But if you ever get a chance to watch it, you should. It's about this couple in Waco who remodel old homes for people. It's amazing what they do. Jade thinks she wants to be an interior designer now, after watching shows on HGTV."

Charlotte smiled. "I'm sure she'd be a great interior designer. She's very artistic, isn't she?"

"Yes. Much better than me. I can't draw much beyond stick figures, you know?"

Charlotte laughed. "Me, neither. So, what else do you two like to watch on TV?"

"Well, we don't have cable anymore so we're pretty limited. It's okay, it's not like we have a lot of time to watch TV, anyway."

Charlotte nodded. "So, do you need cable to watch Fixer Upper?"

"Yes."

"Oh. Well, I'll bet Jade misses it, then."

Lexi shrugged. "Probably. She doesn't complain about it, though."

"No, I'm sure she doesn't. She's pretty happy-go-lucky, isn't she?"

"Not much point in being anything else, is there? It's not like complaining would make any difference."

"Well, that's true."

"I've just got to vacuum now, then I'll be done." Lexi walked out of the apartment and got the vacuum cleaner, leaving the front door open. Charlotte felt a little vulnerable with the door open and was relieved when Lexi returned and closed the door again. As Lexi plugged in the vacuum cleaner, Charlotte got up and walked over by the door. Once Lexi started vacuuming and wasn't paying any attention to Charlotte, she turned and locked the front door, including the dead bolt. She didn't bother with the chain, as she didn't want to alert Lexi to any problems.

A few minutes later, Lexi was winding the cord back onto the vacuum cleaner. "Okay, that's it. I guess we'll see you at five-thirty, Charlotte."

"How will Jade get here, now that your schedule's changed and you don't come together?"

"Jimmy told me he'd drop her off."

"What about on other days? Once she's out of school, and you're working full time, what will Jade do? Does your mother work days, too?"

"No, her schedule's kind of all over the place. Jade will either stay home by herself or come with me and hang out in the park."

"Lexi, you and I need to talk about that."

"What do you mean?"

"I don't think it's safe for Jade to be in the park by herself. Lexi, who is that man with the black pickup?"

"Black pickup?"

"Now, before you say anything else, I know you know who I'm talking about. He tried to get on the bus the other day. I know you two saw him and you looked frightened. So, don't deny it. Please. Who is he?"

Lexi sighed. "You're right, Charlotte. I know who you're talking about. But I really can't do anything about it, you know?"

"Who is he? And why is he bothering you and Jade? I saw him another time, you know."

Lexi looked surprised. "Another time?"

"Yes. At the park. Jade was lying down on the grass with a book over her face, taking a nap. He stood not ten feet from her and stared down at her. He looked menacing. This was before I'd met Jade, by the way. I was sitting on the balcony and then a soccer ball hit the guy in the head and the boys who'd been playing soccer ran over, they all got into a shouting match, and Jade jumped up and ran off."

Lexi seemed to think this over then asked, "So you've seen him twice? Any other times?"

"No, that's it. Just twice. But I'm worried. You have a reason to be afraid of him, don't you?"

Lexi nodded. "You could say that."

"Tell me about it."

"Not now, Charlotte." As Charlotte started to speak up, Lexi interrupted her. "Look, I'll tell you all about it, okay? But not now, I have to get back to work. I've got a bunch of apartments to clean today and I don't want to be late for your surprise. How about if I bring my lunch here, and I'll talk with you about it then?"

Charlotte nodded. "Okay."

"But Charlotte?"

"Yes?"

"If I share a secret with you, then you need to share one with me. That's what friends do, right?"

Charlotte was surprised. "You think I have a secret?"

Lexi laughed. "Oh, Charlotte. I think you have a bunch of secrets. But I'll settle for one."

"One?"

"Yep. I want you to explain your name. Tilian."

"Oh. Well, that's a little complicated. It might involve revealing more than one secret."

"Well, then, that makes me pretty clever, doesn't it?" Lexi had a mischievous grin on her face as she left the apartment.

Chapter 17

After Lexi left, Charlotte made sure the front door was locked and the safety chain secured. She went back to the living room, picked up her phone and saw that she had a voice mail message. She sat to listen to the message.

"Hello, Charlotte. I was very disappointed yesterday when I went by your place and saw the realtor's sign out front. I guess you felt the need to buy a more expensive place with your new-found wealth. I hope you don't get too attached to the new place. I plan to take back what's rightfully mine. I guess you and I weren't the only ones with secrets, right, Charlotte? You and Carla seem to have had your share of secrets, too. Well, we'll talk more when I see you, Charlotte. And yes – I will see you before I leave Houston. You and I have some unfinished business."

A chill went through Charlotte and she started to delete the message but then thought better of it. After all, it may be evidence at some point. So. Think, Charlotte. What would he do next? Charlotte picked up her phone and looked through the contacts. Finding the number she wanted, she placed her call.

"Franklin Realty. How may I direct your call?"

"Hello. Jane, please."

"May I tell her who's calling?"

"Charlotte Tilian."

"Thank you. One moment, please."

Charlotte waited for the woman to come on the line.

"Ms. Tilian! I was just thinking of you."

"Really?"

"Yes! A gentleman called this morning and wants to see your condo. I'm showing it to him at ten-thirty."

"Did he give his name?"

"Let me see. Yes. Dave White. Said he was moving here from New Mexico."

"What a liar," thought Charlotte. Not even a very original liar. Dave White was his brother's name. And visiting his daughter was the closest he'd ever come to living in New Mexico. But all she said to Jane was, "Please cancel the appointment, Jane."

"Cancel it? Ms. Tilian, I hate to do that. We really haven't had many showings lately. He sounded very interested."

"I understand. But the truth is, I've decided to take it off the market."

"Oh! Does your son know about this decision?"

"Not yet. But it's my property, not his. And my decision."

"Well, yes, of course. So, are you moving back to the condo? The retirement home not working out for you?"

"It's complicated, Jane. Do I need to sign any paperwork? If so, I'm not in Houston right now, I'm in Denver, visiting my daughter. I've already moved out of the retirement community. So, I can't run by your office any time soon."

"Well, I'll e-mail something to you."

"That will be great. Thank you."

She ended the call. She hoped the lie about being in Denver would buy her some time if "Dave" tried to weasel information from Jane about where she was living. Of course, she knew how charming he could be, and he could still manage to learn from Jane where she had moved to after she'd moved out of her condo. Then he'd come snooping around here. She wished she hadn't made the plans for to-night, now, but she wasn't about to change them. There was no way she would disappoint Lexi and Jade; she suspected they'd had enough disappointment in their young lives.

The doorbell buzzed and she couldn't help but be anxious about who it might be. She looked out the peephole and saw Peter standing at her door, holding a small package. Oh, good! She opened the door.

"Hello, Ms. Tilian. You received this package. I thought I'd save you a trip downstairs."

"Why, thank you, Peter, that's very kind of you. Just a moment."

76

She found her handbag and pulled out a five-dollar bill. "Here you are. Thanks again."

Peter handed the package to her, told her to have a nice day, and closed the door behind him as he left. She locked, bolted, and chained the door and took the package into her bedroom. She found a small gift bag and blank note card in her closet then opened the package and inspected the necklace. It looked even prettier than she'd expected. She hoped Lexi would like it. She placed the necklace in the gift bag, added some tissue paper, and wrote a note in the card. Thank goodness for online shopping!

Charlotte glanced at the clock on her nightstand. Lexi should be here, soon. She made her way to the kitchen and put the kettle on; she'd make a pitcher of iced tea for lunch. Not knowing what Lexi would bring for her lunch, Charlotte decided to make a salad. It would be enough for her own lunch, plus Lexi could have some, too if she wanted. She started pulling items out of the fridge and started thinking about how to tell Lexi about her name. As she washed lettuce and chopped vegetables, her thoughts turned to her past. She didn't like looking back, she preferred looking forward. Just as she set the salad on the kitchen table, the doorbell buzzed again. She went to the door and looked out; it was Lexi. Show time.

Chapter 18

Lexi and Charlotte sat across from each other at the small kitchen table. Lexi took her sandwich out of her sack and took a bite. Charlotte nodded at the salad bowl. "There's plenty of salad, if you'd like some."

"Sure. Thanks." Lexi helped herself to the salad, added some dressing and took a sip of tea. "This is good iced tea. Sweet, but not too sweet."

Charlotte nodded. "Thank you. So, did you have a lot of apartments to clean this morning?"

Lexi nodded. "Yes. And that old guy in four-o-one, his place is always a mess. I don't understand how one person can get a place so dirty in just a few days."

"Pretty bad, huh?"

"Yes. He doesn't even rinse off his dishes. Just piles them all up in the sink for me to clean twice a week. It's disgusting. Dirty clothes and towels all over the bathroom floor. Never makes his bed. I guess it just gets made on the two days I show up to clean. *And* he has a cat and I'm the only one who ever changes the litter box. It's just gross."

Charlotte made a face. "Sounds like it." She looked at Lexi. "So. The guy with the black pickup."

Lexi sighed. "Yeah." She put down her salad fork and looked up at Charlotte.

"What do you know about me and Jade, Charlotte?"

"Know about you?"

Lexi shrugged. "Yeah. I mean, based on what people have told you or you've observed. What do you know about us?"

"Well, nobody has told me anything about you. Who would? So, all I know is what you've told me or, as you say, what I've observed."

"Which is?"

"You just graduated from high school, you're eighteen years old. You're a good student – oh, I was wrong, somebody did tell me about you – Mrs. Lewis."

Lexi nodded. "And?"

"Your parents don't seem very involved in your life – at least, not your school life. You work here and you try very hard to take care of your eleven-year-old sister. Sometimes you ride your bike to work, sometimes you ride the bus. You do have neighbors who help you out from time-to-time but I've never heard you mention any friends around your age. You aren't real chatty, you don't like to talk about yourself, and you have a strong work ethic. You're a woman of strong character, resilient, respectful and caring of others. You enjoy reading and you have dreams of a better future. And the ability to achieve those dreams."

Lexi seemed surprised by Charlotte's assessment of her, and somewhat embarrassed. Then she said, "And I'm poor. I live in a bad neighborhood. You knew that, right?"

"Based on what I've observed, I'd be surprised if your family is wealthy. I have no idea where you live."

"Okay, here's a quick bio. We live in a Section Eight apartment with my mom, though she's in and out a lot so it's usually just me and Jade. My dad left when I was three and I really don't remember him. I have no idea where he is. Jade's dad never lived with us. He shows up once in a while and takes her to McDonalds for a little father-daughter bonding. He's never paid child support, as far as I know.

I can't remember a time when my mother wasn't strung out on something – booze, drugs, men. She's a mess. Oh, she's had her moments. She's been to rehab twice, and has had a few weeks here and there when she was sober. She's been to jail a lot, mostly for stuff like public intox and prostitution, but also a couple more serious charges."

Lexi paused, as if to note Charlotte's reaction. When Charlotte nodded, she continued.

"So, anyway, a few months ago, this creep, Dennis started hanging around a lot. She met him at an N.A. meeting and supposedly, they were in love and were gonna help each other stay straight. They're both on probation, so they really shouldn't be hanging out together. But he practically moved in with us for a while.

At first, it wasn't too bad. They'd go to their meetings, he had a job and she was off the streets. But he could be mean, too. They started to fight a lot."

"Did it get physical?"

"Not at first. Mostly a lot of yelling and slamming of doors. He'd take off and be gone a few days, then come back, they'd make up for a while, that sort of thing."

"How did he treat you and Jade?"

"Mostly, he ignored us. He'd complain to Regina – my mom – about stuff, like how much we ate, that we didn't show him respect, that kind of thing.

Anyway, they didn't stay sober very long. Soon, I was the only one working and things were tight. One morning, I got up and went into the kitchen to fix breakfast for Jade and me. Charlotte, there was literally nothing to eat. I don't mean there was stuff to eat, but nothing that we liked, I mean there was *nothing* to eat. Then I walked into the living room and they were both passed out. Not just sleeping, passed out. The room was a mess. Empty beer cans, overflowing ash trays, roach clips; you get the picture. There was a baggy of pot on the table, which was almost empty. Then I saw the coke."

"Cocaine?"

Lexi nodded. "Yep. I was livid. I mean, we had *no food* in the house, Charlotte. Nothing! But they can buy beer and drugs and get high while I'm the only one with a job? It infuriated me. Now, Charlotte, this is the part where I have to really trust you. You'd have to keep a secret about me that you may not want to keep. Do you want me to keep going?"

Charlotte didn't answer right away. She wanted Lexi to know she took her question seriously. She wondered what Lexi was about to tell her but she sensed Lexi needed to unburden herself of this secret.

Besides, who was she to judge anyone? Of course, Charlotte would keep her secret. So, she told her to continue.

"Okay, then. I woke up Jade, and told her we needed to leave earlier than usual so she could eat breakfast at school. While she was getting dressed, I put the coke in my backpack. I told her to ride the bike to school and I walked in the opposite direction, toward my school. But once she was out of sight, I changed direction. I ended up going somewhere I knew I could unload the coke. And I sold it, Charlotte. So, I'm a drug dealer. Scum of the earth, that's me. A low-life drug dealer."

"How much did you get for it?"

"A lot."

"And what did you do with the money?"

"I hid most of it. I bought groceries. That's it."

"And I guess Dennis is after you because he figured out you took the drugs."

"Yeah. I didn't go to school or work that day but stayed away until the time I'd normally get home. Nobody was there and later, while Jade and I were eating dinner, Tamara came over to tell us Regina was in jail for a probation violation. She'd tested positive on a drug test. Jade was pretty upset."

"I can imagine."

"Anyway, the next morning, we're getting ready for school and the asshole shows up."

"You let him in?"

"He had a key."

"Ah."

"Yeah. Anyway, he started screaming at me, wanting to know what I did with his stuff. Jade walked out of the bathroom to see what was going on and he grabbed her but she slipped out of his grasp and ran out of the apartment. He slammed me up against a wall and had my arm twisted behind my back. He was twisting it so hard, I thought I was gonna pass out. But then Jimmy showed up."

"Jade had gotten him?"

81

"Yes, ma'am. Anyway, he told Dennis in no uncertain terms to get out and not come back. Well, Jimmy's a little guy and Dennis is really big so I guess he figured Jimmy wasn't a threat. So, he laughed at Jimmy, which really pissed Jimmy off. Then Jimmy pulled out a gun."

"Oh, my."

Lexi nodded. "Yeah, it was pretty intense. But Dennis left. He told us he was gonna kill all of us if he didn't have his shit back in twenty-four hours."

"Did you call the police?"

"No. Jimmy's a convicted felon, on probation, so he sure didn't want the cops involved. You know – the gun. I didn't want to have to explain what I'd done with the cocaine. So, we agreed we wouldn't call the cops. Jimmy and Tamara had us stay with them for a couple of days. He took me to the emergency room that morning, after we dropped Jade off at school. My arm wasn't broken, just sprained, so I wore a sling and missed a couple of days from school."

"That must have been tough for Jade, going to school after everything that happened that morning."

"Well, we aren't exactly the Brady Bunch, Charlotte. It's not like she isn't used to turmoil."

"So, has Dennis come back to your apartment?"

"I don't know. I haven't seen him. Jimmy changed the locks for us that day, so at least he doesn't have a key. Jimmy and some of his buddies keep an eye out for him. But he does stalk us sometimes, like the two times you saw him. So far, he hasn't hurt us. I think he may have been in jail for a while, or something, 'cuz until recently, we hadn't seen him for a couple of months."

"Maybe so. And your mom? How long was she in jail?"

"About a month, I guess. Then she had a hearing, agreed to go to rehab again, and they continued her on probation. But when she got out of rehab this time, she didn't stay clean at all. Right back to using, doing tricks for drugs, just like always. She's had a couple of positive drug tests and figures she's going to prison soon. That's what I was doing Saturday; I was helping her try to find Jade's dad. She's hoping if she goes to prison, he'll take care of Jade. Otherwise, she'll probably end up in foster care. We've been there, done that, and believe me, we don't want that to happen again."

"Well, since you're eighteen, couldn't she stay with you?"

"I don't know. Maybe. I said the same thing to Regina but she says that son-of-a-bitch, Eddie, needs to step up and be a father." Lexi laughed. "Like she's mother of the year."

"Did you find him?"

"No. Not yet."

"So now what?"

"I don't know, Charlotte. Regina was picked up yesterday. And I have no idea what to do next. Any ideas?"

"Well, I'll do whatever I can to help. Let me do some checking this afternoon."

"Really?"

"Of course. So, I guess the note from your mom…"

"Oh, she did write it, Charlotte. She's probably hoping you're some rich old woman she can use, somehow."

"Or maybe she just wanted you and Jade to have fun this evening."

Lexi rolled her eyes. "Yeah, right. Now, it's your turn, Charlotte. Tell me about the Tilian name."

Charlotte checked the time. "Well, we only have about ten minutes before you have to get back to work. So, I'll give you the short version now, and the details later, okay?"

"Okay."

"Lexi, I've made many mistakes in my life. For a time, I probably had more in common with your mother than you'd guess. That's the part I'll tell you about later. Let's just say I wasn't "mother of the year," either."

Lexi didn't react, just took a sip of tea and motioned for her to continue.

"Anyway, after years of being a total screw-up, I turned my life around. Got sober, went to college, started paying attention to my children - two of whom were grown by then - got a job, and started writing. At one point, I started thinking about my name. I was divorced and using an ex-husband's name. I didn't feel right about that and considered using my maiden name. But that didn't feel right, either.

I was finally standing on my own two feet and I didn't want anyone else's name — not my father's, not my mother's, not a husband's. So, I decided I would create my own name. After all, words were my world, right? I was a poet, surely I could come up with a name for myself."

"That's pretty cool."

"You think so? You don't think it was crazy?"

"No. In fact, maybe I'll do that someday. Once I figure out who I am."

Charlotte smiled.

"Charlotte, it reminds me of the woman who wrote the book about walking the Pacific Crest Trail — there was a movie based on the book, too. Cheryl something-or-other."

"Strayed. Cheryl Strayed."

"Yeah. Like her. She chose her own last name, right? Anyway, I like the idea."

"Well, I'm glad you understand."

"So, why Tilian?"

"Well, up until then, most people called me Charlie, a nickname I'd been given as a child. Then I discovered Charlotte means "free woman" and I decided to let go of Charlie; it seemed too youthful and innocent, anyway. I liked the meaning behind Charlotte and wanted something meaningful to pair with it. Tilian means "strives." And I realized that was a good way to define myself and the type of life I wanted to lead — someone who was always striving. To be better, to do better, to achieve a deeper understanding of all life has to offer and the people I meet along the way. I didn't want to ever settle or be satisfied with my life the way it was, again. I wanted to always strive for self-improvement. So, it resonated with me. I chose it as my name. I also liked the sound of it, you know? Charlotte Tilian." She smiled.

Lexi smiled, too. "It does sound pretty. But strong, too, not just pretty."

"Exactly. Now, you'd better get going. You don't want to be late getting back from your lunch break."

Lexi stood and started to clear the table but Charlotte shooed her off, telling her she'd take care of the dishes. She thanked Charlotte for lunch then reached for her hand and held it tightly.

"Charlotte, thank you. Not just for lunch, but for being my friend. It means a lot to me."

Charlotte smiled and reached out to hug her. "Dear child, our friendship means a lot to me, too."

"Even though I'm a terrible person?"

"Terrible person?!"

Lexi pulled away from Charlotte and looked down at her feet. "You know…the drugs."

Charlotte shook her head. "You are not a terrible person. Do I wish you hadn't sold the drugs you found that morning? Sure. But mostly out of fear of what could have happened to you. I think you were a young person put into a situation you never should have had to face in the first place, and you just dealt with it the best way you knew how at the time. You were angry and hurt, and you had a right to be. Now that you've had time to consider your actions, I think you see it wasn't the right thing to have done. But you can't undo the past, Lexi. Just don't make the same mistake again. Don't let one mistake define you. You are a good person."

Lexi shrugged.

"Look at me, Lexi."

She looked up. "Yes, ma'am."

"You are a good person. With a wonderful life ahead of you. Okay?"

"Okay."

"Good. Now go on, I don't want you to be late."

As she left, Lexi turned and smiled at Charlotte before closing the front door behind her. Charlotte locked up and returned to the kitchen to clean up the lunch dishes.

Chapter 19

After cleaning up in the kitchen, Charlotte went to her desk and started to log in to the computer. But then, she thought about someone who might be able to help. She made a call but was told the person she needed to speak with wasn't there but would be available the next day. She hung up and a couple of minutes later, her phone rang. It was John. Charlotte sighed, braced herself mentally, and took the call.

"Hello, John. How are you?"

"Mom! What the heck is going on?"

"I guess Jane called you."

"Damn right, she did and it's a good thing, too. What the hell are you thinking? And what are you doing in Denver? Is Julie there with you now?"

"Calm down, John. I'm not in Denver."

"Well, what the heck was Jane talking about then?"

"Look, I was just trying to mislead her about my location, that's all."

"That's all? Mom, what is going on?"

"Well, it's a long story."

"I've got all day."

She sighed. What should she tell him? Just enough of the truth to satisfy his curiosity, but not so much that he'd come running to Houston. "Okay. Well. You remember my friend, Carla?"

There was a pause. "Carla? The woman who lives in Philadelphia? The one you used to take vacations with, that woman?"

"Yes. Carla White. Well, she passed away recently."

"I'm sorry, Mom. But what does that have to do with any of this?"

"Well, I was talking with her daughter, and she told me that her father – Carla's husband – was in Houston and wanted to visit me."

"Uh huh."

"John, he's a horrible man. I don't want to see him. And I don't want him to know where I am. According to their daughter, he still thinks I live on Clay Street. I think it's best if he continues to think that. I figure he'll go by a couple of times, give up, and go home to Philadelphia. I don't want to see him."

"So, why lie to Jane? Why take the house off the market? And Mom, is this guy dangerous? Shouldn't you be talking to the police, if he is? Do you want me to call him? Or come to Houston? And why didn't you tell me about any of this? Mom, how on earth can I take care of you if you won't tell me what the hell is going on in your life?"

By this time, he was practically screaming. "John, calm down. It isn't anything that the police need to be involved in. If it was, I would have called them. I just don't like him, that's all. I was afraid he'd see the sign in the yard and call Jane and weasel my current address out of her. So, I told her to take the house off the market and made up the story about being out of town. Once I know he's back in Philadelphia, I'll call Jane, don't worry."

"Mom, this whole story sounds crazy. Why not just be honest with Jane? She won't disclose any information about you."

"John, you don't know the man like I do. Jane would be no match for him. Hell, he'd probably talk her into driving him here to see me. I like Jane, but honestly, John, she's not the sharpest tool in the shed, is she?"

He sighed. "Okay, I'll give you that. But Mom, this isn't one of your novels, we don't need all this intrigue. From now on, will you please keep me in the loop? And call me if you need anything?"

"Of course I will. Now, how are you? Still playing a lot of golf?"

"A little, yeah. We're planning a trip to Alaska. One of those cruises. Which is another reason I need to know you're okay. I don't want to leave if you're going to need me."

"Oh, John, I'm fine. Don't worry so much. I have plenty of friends here and I can always call Julie or Heather if I need anything. But I won't. I've finished my physical therapy and I'm feeling stronger every day. I see my doctor next week and I'm going to ask him about driving."

"Driving? Mom, are you sure you're ready to drive already?"

"Maybe. I'll talk it over with the doctor first, don't worry."

"What about the walker? Are you still using it?"

"No, I quit using that some time ago. I move a little slow, but I do okay without it."

"Well, be careful. You don't want to fall and break a hip or something."

"I know."

"Well, okay then. I'm going to call you every day until that guy goes back to Philadelphia, just to make sure you're okay. Alright?"

"Sure, that's fine. Thank you, John. Please don't say anything to Jane, though, okay?"

"I won't. Your secret's safe with me, Mom."

"Good. Well, take care. I love you."

"Love you too, Mom. Bye."

Well. So much for being a "free woman." John made her feel like a helpless child. She knew he meant well, but honestly, sometimes it was just too much.

A couple hours later, the doorbell buzzed and Charlotte went to the door. She looked out the peephole and saw Jade standing at the door.

"Hello, Jade. How was school?"

Jade entered the apartment. "Hi, Ms. T. It was okay. How are you?"

"I'm well, thank you. Come on in. Would you like a little snack?"

"No, thank you. But maybe a glass of water?"

"Sure. Come on back to the kitchen."

They walked back to the kitchen, Jade set her backpack down, and Charlotte pulled a glass down from a cupboard. She handed it to Jade, who filled it with ice and water from the refrigerator door.

"Thank you."

"You're welcome."

"Did Lexi bring our clothes for tonight?"

"Yes, she did. Do you want to go ahead and get ready? Or do you have homework?"

"No homework. Today was our last real day of school. I have to go tomorrow but it's just half a day, and we won't really do anything. Just our final assembly, really."

"Oh. What happens at the assembly?"

"The principal gives a speech and the choir sings a couple of songs. Then they hand out awards. After that, we get to go home."

"What kind of awards?"

"Attendance. Academic achievement. Sports. All kinds of stuff."

"Do parents attend?"

"Some do, yeah."

"Can anyone attend?"

Jade shrugged. "I guess so. Some kids' grandparents come, and little brothers and sisters. My friend, Sam's grandpa is coming. She's all excited about it, 'cuz he's visiting from New York and she's probably gonna get an award, she's really smart."

"That's nice. Do you have grandparents, Jade?"

She frowned. "I don't think so. Lexi had a grandma who was always real nice to me and let me call her grandma. But she died. I don't know of any others."

"I'm sorry to hear that. When did she die?"

"Mmmm, let's see, it was just before Christmas, year before last."

"So, she was Lexi's paternal grandmother, if she wasn't your biological grandmother, right?"

"Paternal?"

"Her dad's mother."

"Oh. Yes. That's right. Regina's mom died a long time ago. I was real little when she died. She died in a car accident. A drunk driver hit her car."

90

"That's awful."

"I know. She wasn't very old, either, not like most kids' grand-mas."

"Jade, how old is your mom?"

"Regina?"

Charlotte nodded.

"She's thirty-five."

"Thirty-five? Are you sure?"

"Yes, ma'am, why?"

"No reason, really. I'm just thinking she's pretty young to have an eighteen-year-old daughter."

"I know. She was in high school when she got pregnant. She quit school. She's always telling us not to make the same mistake she did. Like we would. That was dumb, quitting school."

"Well, I think now it may be a little easier for a pregnant girl to stay in school. It used to be frowned upon, and girls had to quit or go to a special school. Maybe that's how it was for your mom."

She shrugged. "Maybe. I just know I wouldn't quit school."

Charlotte smiled. "I'm glad to hear it. So, let me show you where your clothes are, and you can go ahead and get ready. I have some wonderful bubble bath, if you'd like to take a bath."

"Really? I love bubble baths!"

"I thought you might."

After showing Jade where everything was, Charlotte left her in her bathroom and closed the door, as well as the bedroom door so Jade could have privacy to get dressed for this evening. Charlotte sat in the living room and read while she waited on her. A little later, she heard the bedroom door open and looked back to see Jade walking toward her.

"Do I look okay, Ms. T?"

"Jade, you look beautiful! I love that color on you!"

She beamed. "Thank you. Is this dressy enough?"

"It's perfect. Now, have a seat. I know you probably want to watch your home decorating shows. I'm going to go get ready now. Will you be okay on your own for a bit?"

"Sure. I'll just watch TV while I wait."

"Okay. Now if anyone comes to the door, unless it's Lexi, just don't answer it, okay?"

"Yes, ma'am."

"Good. I won't be long."

"No problem. Are you gonna have a bubble bath, too? 'Cuz it sure was nice, it smelled yumptious."

Charlotte laughed. "You know, I think I will."

Chapter 20

Shortly after Charlotte was ready, the doorbell buzzed. It was Lexi. She got ready, too and by 6:15, the three of them were ready to go.

"Ms. T, is Lexi driving us to the surprise?" asked Jade.

"No, she isn't."

"I'm not?" asked Lexi in surprise. "Is the van taking us?"

"No."

"Are you driving?"

"No."

"Oh. So, we're taking the bus?"

Charlotte could see the disappointment on Lexi's face and laughed. "No. Quit asking questions, it's all part of the surprise." She grabbed her handbag, which was large enough to hide the gift bag. "Let's go."

The girls looked at each other with expressions on their faces like, "What the heck is this crazy old lady up to?" They took the elevator down to the lobby and as they were passing the reception desk, Peter motioned to Charlotte. She turned to Lexi and Jade. "Girls, wait here. I need to speak with Peter for a moment." She walked over toward Peter and he smiled nervously at her. "Good evening, Ms. Tilian."

"Hello, Peter. Is everything okay?"

"I just wanted you to know that the gentleman in the photos came by about an hour ago."

"An hour ago?!"

"Yes, ma'am. I apologize that I wasn't able to contact you earlier. But he left and then I was very busy. I was just about to come up and tell you about it, when I saw you get off the elevator."

"Well, what did he say? And what did you tell him?"

"He asked which apartment you lived in. At first, I acted as if I didn't know who he was talking about. Then he showed me your picture. I said, 'Oh, yes. I remember her. She doesn't live here anymore. She had a stroke and was moved to a nursing home.'"

"Did he buy it?"

"Yes, I think so. He asked which nursing home and I told him I didn't know. He asked if I could find out and I asked how he knew you. He said he was an old family friend. I told him I couldn't disclose information to him, since he isn't family, and I suggested he contact your children. He said he would do that, and left."

"Did you see him leave the grounds?"

"Yes, he had a cab and left in it. Ms. Tilian, are you sure you're safe? He didn't seem like a very nice man. Would you like me to call the police?"

"No, no, it's fine. You did great, Peter, thank you. I'm sure he won't be back."

"It's my pleasure, Ms. Tilian. Oh, it looks as if your limo is here."

She looked over, and saw the limousine through the glass doors of the building. "Yes, I think you're right."

"Have a nice evening, Ms. Tilian."

"Thank you, Peter."

She walked back over to the girls. "Come on, girls. I believe our ride is here."

The look on their faces was priceless. Their eyes got huge and their mouths gaped in surprise. "This limo is for us?!" Jade squealed.

"Yes, it is. Have you ever ridden in a limo?"

"Are you kidding?! No way! Come, on Lexi!" Jade grabbed Lexi's hand and hurried out the doors to the limo.

Once they were all settled in, the driver pulled away from the building and headed toward downtown. The girls were checking out everything in the car.

"This is so cool, Ms. T! Can we have one of those cokes?"

"Of course. Help yourself."

The girls each grabbed a coke. Jade held one up to her. "Would you like a coke, Ms. T?"

"That sounds pretty good. Thank you." Charlotte accepted the drink and smiled at the girls. They were so excited.

"Do you use limos a lot, Ms. T?" asked Lexi.

"Oh, no. Just special occasions. Probably less than five times in my entire life. I think it would be less special if you did it a lot, wouldn't it?"

"Less special and pretty expensive."

Charlotte laughed. "That, too."

"So, what's the special occasion?" asked Jade.

"Why, your sister's graduation from high school, of course."

Jade beamed. "She was an honor graduate, Ms. T."

"Really?"

Jade nodded. "She ranked number twelve in her class."

"That's outstanding!" Charlotte replied.

Lexi shrugged. "It's not like valedictorian, or anything. No big deal."

"It's a very big deal, Lexi. Congratulations."

Lexi looked uncomfortable with the compliment but said, "Thanks."

"Where are we going, Ms. T?" asked Jade. "Are we going out to dinner? In a fancy restaurant? Is that why you wanted us to dress up?"

"Would you like that?"

"Oh, yes! The only place we ever go out to eat is McDonald's or Golden Corral. We aren't going there, are we? I mean, if we are, it's okay…"

"Not tonight, Jade. I admit Golden Corral sounds tempting, but I have other plans tonight."

Jade smiled and looked out the window. "It's really cool how there are all those cars and people out there and we can't even hear them. Can they see us?"

"No, the windows are tinted, so though you can see out, they can't see us."

"Cool. I kinda wish they could see us, though. They'd think we were celebrities, or something."

"Well, roll down the window, if you want."

"Can I?"

"Sure!"

"Can I do the 'queen wave' to people?"

Lexi rolled her eyes. "Jade, really? Don't do that."

But Jade pushed the button to roll down her window and looked out. A few people glanced at her and she smiled and waved. She didn't do the "queen wave," though, she waved excitedly, like the happy little girl she was at that moment. Charlotte loved seeing her so happy. Even Lexi smiled.

Chapter 21

As they stepped out of the limousine, Jade looked over toward the glass tower of the hotel. "Look, Ms. T! There's an elevator on the outside of that tower! Look how high it goes!"

"I know. Looks like fun, doesn't it?"

Jade nodded. "What's at the top?"

"Let's find out, shall we?"

Jade's eyes grew wide. "Really?! We're riding on that elevator?"

Charlotte nodded and reached for her hand. "Come on." The three of them rode the glass elevator the thirty-four stories to the Spindletop Restaurant, high above downtown Houston. The girls seemed in awe as they looked out over the city. As they stepped off, Jade asked if they would get to ride the elevator again when they left.

"Of course. I don't think I'm up to walking down thirty-four flights of stairs."

"Me, neither," Jade responded seriously.

Once they were seated and had their drinks, the girls pondered the menus for quite a while.

"Does anything look good?" Charlotte asked.

Lexi spoke up. "Oh, yes, ma'am, everything looks delicious. But Jade and I really don't eat big dinners. Maybe we could just share a meal."

It occurred to Charlotte they were nervous about the prices. "Oh, no. How about we each order something different? That way, we can get an idea of what all they have to offer, in case you want to come back again sometime. If you can't eat it all, that's okay. You can even take a doggie bag home, if you like."

The girls looked at each other. Finally, Lexi looked around then quietly asked, "Charlotte, are those numbers after each meal, the prices? Because if they are, you know this place is really expensive, right?"

Charlotte nodded. "Those are the prices, Lexi. But don't worry about it. You order whatever you want. Heck, order two meals, if you want! This is a special occasion and we're going to do it up right. In fact, I think we should start with an appetizer. Which one sounds good to you girls?"

"Ms. T, did you see that they have octopus salad?" Jade shook her head. "That sounds gross."

Charlotte smiled. "Maybe we'll avoid that."

Lexi asked, "How about the stuffed peppers? Would that be a good appetizer?"

"It sounds good to me. Jade, what do you think?"

"Sure. Sounds good."

"Okay. Now, what about the meals?"

"What are you going to have, Charlotte?" asked Lexi.

"I think I'll have the glazed salmon."

"I'm going to have the ravioli," announced Jade, as she closed her menu.

"Okay. You did notice it has shrimp and crawfish tails with it, right? Do you like that?"

Jade shrugged. "I won't know 'til I try it."

"That's the spirit! Lexi, what will you have?"

"I think the grilled chicken breast sounds good."

The waitress came over and took their orders then they chatted and enjoyed the view.

"This is really cool, how the restaurant moves around so the view changes. But it moves so slow, you really don't feel like you're moving, do you?" asked Jade.

Charlotte nodded in agreement. "I think you'll enjoy the view even more as it starts to get dark and all of the lights come on in the city. It's really quite beautiful."

"Do you come here a lot?" asked Jade.

"No. I've been here a couple of times. I think it's a nice place to come for special occasions."

"It's really nice, Charlotte. Thanks for bringing us here," said Lexi.

The appetizer arrived and they enjoyed the peppers while continuing to visit.

"So, what's your schedule like tomorrow, girls?"

Lexi answered. "Well, I work all day tomorrow. Jade has school. She has to be there by seven-thirty and they get out early, since it's the last day. Eleven-thirty, right, Jade?"

Jade nodded but didn't answer, since her mouth was full.

"So, since she has to be at school by seven-thirty, we'll leave the house a little after seven. I'll walk with her to school, then ride my bike the rest of the way to work. I'll get there a little early, so I'll probably sit in the dining room and have some coffee before I start my shift."

"And what will Jade do after school?"

"She'll walk home. Tamara said she could hang out with their kids until I get home."

"And what about the assembly?"

"What about it?" asked Jade.

"Will anyone be there for you? I mean, what if you get an award?"

"Oh. Well, I am getting an award, I'm pretty sure. Maybe more than one. But what about it?"

"Will you have any family there to see you get the award?"

"Oh. No. But my friends and my teachers will be there. It's okay, Ms. T. It's no big deal."

"May I come?"

Jade looked surprised. "You wanna come to the assembly?"

"Yes. If it's okay with you."

Jade shrugged and tried to look nonchalant but there was a hint of a smile on her face. She looked down at the stuffed pepper on her plate. "I guess it's okay. If you really want to, I mean."

"I do really want to." Charlotte handed her phone to Lexi. "Can you enter the name and address of the school for me, please?"

"Sure. This is really nice of you, Charlotte. You need to be sure and take an I.D. with you and you'll have to sign it at the office."

"What time is the assembly?"

"I'm not sure. You could probably call the school in the morning and ask, though."

"Okay. Is there any way you could attend, too? Any way to get off work for a bit?"

Lexi shook her head. "No, ma'am. I can't just take off at the last minute. Plus, I really need to work, you know?"

Charlotte nodded. "Of course." She turned to Jade. "Well, I will definitely plan to attend. It's been a long time since I've attended a school assembly. It should be fun."

Jade smiled back at her.

"And then, how about you spend the afternoon with me? Or would you rather spend it with Tamara's kids?"

Jade looked over at Lexi. "Can I, Lexi? Please?"

"Charlotte, are you sure? Do you really want to spend all day with Jade tomorrow, after spending time with us tonight? You're gonna get sick of us."

Charlotte disagreed. "Probably the other way around. You girls may already be sick of this old woman."

"Oh, no, Ms. T! We love you! You're awesome."

"Why, thank you, Jade. So, it's settled. In fact, if you think it would be alright with your mother, you're welcome to spend the night at my apartment. You girls could sleep in my bedroom and I'll take the couch. We could even run by your place and pick up a change of clothes for you on the way home."

Lexi thought it over. "Well, I don't think it would be a good idea to take a limo to our neighborhood. But if you're sure it's okay, we could do that and if you don't mind, just use your washer and drier tonight. I could wash my work clothes from today and wear them tomorrow. Jade could wear what she's wearing tonight, and that way she'll look nice for the assembly tomorrow. But we aren't kicking you out of your bedroom. We'll sleep in the living room."

100

Charlotte decided not to argue with Lexi over the sleeping arrangements. She was just relieved Lexi had agreed they could stay with her tonight as she was really worried about them being alone with that Dennis creep on the loose. Even with the situation she was dealing with herself, she felt they were safer at her apartment than being on their own. So, she just nodded and said that sounded like a good plan.

After the dinner plates were cleared, the waitress approached their table. "Can I interest you in one of our fine desserts, ladies?"

"Of course!" Charlotte responded, before the girls could answer. "Tonight is a special occasion, so we definitely need dessert. And how about something bubbly but non-alcoholic, of course."

The waitress smiled and handed out dessert menus. "We can definitely do that. I highly recommend our banana pudding, by the way. Better than grandma used to make! And what's the special occasion? A birthday?"

Jade piped up, "No, ma'am, my sister graduated from high school!"

"Well, that is a special occasion. Congratulations!"

Lexi smiled and thanked her. "Do you need a moment to look over the menus, or are you ready to order?"

Charlotte looked at the girls and Jade responded, "I think I'd like to have the Nutella-Cream Cheese Brownie, please."

"Excellent choice."

Lexi and Charlotte both decided on the banana pudding and the waitress left. A few minutes later the drinks and desserts arrived and Charlotte made a toast to Lexi. "And four years from now, we'll toast your college graduation!" she announced.

Jade's eyes grew wide. "You're going to college, Lexi?"

Lexi shrugged. "I don't know. Maybe. We'll see."

"You won't go to a college far away and leave me, will you? What will I do, Lexi?"

Jade seemed genuinely alarmed. Oh dear.

But Lexi replied, "Dude. Don't be dumb. If I go to college, it will be the community college here in Houston. I'll just take a couple of classes and keep working, and it will be just like now, okay? I'm not leaving you."

Jade looked relieved. "Oh. I thought when people went to college they moved far away."

"Not always. Rich people, maybe. Not people like us."

Jade nodded. "Well, then I'm glad we're not rich."

Lexi laughed. "Okay."

Charlotte reached into her handbag, pulled out the small gift bag, and handed it to Lexi. "Happy graduation, Lexi."

Lexi's eyes grew wide. "A present?! Charlotte! This is too much."

"Oh, don't be silly. Open it."

Jade smiled. "Yeah, Lexi. Open it. Let's see what it is."

Lexi pulled out the card first and read it. Jade reached for it. "Let me see."

Lexi handed the card to Jade, who read the card and looked up at Charlotte. "That's really nice, Ms. Charlotte."

Charlotte just smiled and watched Lexi open the small box. "Oh, wow. This is so pretty. Look, Jade – a necklace with a seventeen charm." She pulled the necklace out of the box and held it up for Jade to see.

"Aww…that's for the year, right, Lexi? 'Cuz you graduated in twenty-seventeen?"

Lexi nodded. "Thank you so much, Charlotte. How on earth did you find something like this?"

"The wonders of online shopping, Lexi."

As Lexi put the necklace on, Charlotte instructed, "Now, you two girls sit close together, and I'll take your picture."

They posed and she took their picture, then Jade asked if she could take one of Lexi and Charlotte together. As she was taking the photograph, the waitress came back over and asked if they'd like for her to take one of the three of them together. So, they posed and she took the photo. They looked at it and Jade exclaimed at how pretty it was. Then she held up the phone and took a selfie with Charlotte.

Charlotte asked the waitress for the check.

"Oh, no bill tonight, ma'am."

"Excuse me?!"

"A gentleman paid your bill. He's sitting right over there." She turned to point but frowned. "Well, he was right over there at that table. He said he's an old friend and he wanted to surprise you."

Charlotte felt a chill come over her. "What did he look like?"

"Well, let's see…he was probably a little older than you. White hair. A mustache. Real distinguished looking."

"Did he pay with a credit card? Do you recall his name?"

"Actually, he paid with cash. Is everything okay? You look upset."

"I'm fine." She managed to compose herself and smile at the waitress. "I'd just like to know who to thank for this lovely meal, that's all."

"So, you don't have any idea who it was?"

She shook her head. "No, I'm afraid not."

Jade spoke up. "Maybe it was a fan, Ms. T." She looked up at the waitress. "She's a famous author. Charlotte Tilian."

The waitress looked at Charlotte. "No way! How cool! I've read some of your poetry. My English Lit professor last semester loves your stuff and assigned it to our class."

Lexi spoke up. "You're in college?"

The waitress nodded. "Yes. I go to Lone Star College. I'm working on an associate degree in International Studies."

Jade said, "That sounds more interesting than being a waitress. Even in a fancy place like this."

"I hope so."

"That's a community college, right?" asked Lexi. "I mean, a two-year deal?"

"Yes. I'll transfer somewhere else next year. It's okay, and it's cheaper to do it this way."

Lexi nodded. "That's probably what I'll try to do."

"Well, you have lots of choices around here. There's HCC, too."

As the girls spoke with the waitress, Charlotte's thoughts turned to him. He'd been here! In this restaurant, watching them, and she hadn't even noticed. She'd let her guard down. Now what? He must have followed them, so now he knew where she was living, and that she wasn't in Denver, visiting Julie, or in a nursing home. How could she keep herself – and the girls – safe? Maybe John was right, and she should involve the police. But what could they do? And what if the press got wind of it? She sure didn't want her personal business out there, for the world to read. She needed a plan.

Chapter 22

As the limo pulled out of the driveway, Charlotte looked around but didn't see him anywhere. Jade was talking excitedly about the evening. "Which part do you think was best, Ms. T?"

"Hmm?"

"About tonight? The limo, the elevator, the revolving restaurant, the food? I can't decide! Oh, and there's the gift you gave Lexi. This was the best day, ever! And even before we came here – I mean, that bubble bath was awesome! I wish you were our grandma, Ms. T! Hey, do you have any grandkids?"

Lexi shushed Jade. "Don't be nosey, Jade."

"Why? What's wrong with asking about grandkids?"

Charlotte interrupted before Lexi could answer. "There's nothing wrong with asking about grandkids, Jade. I do have three grandchildren. But they live far away and I don't see them very often, I'm afraid."

"That's sad. I bet they miss you. How old are they?"

She closed her eyes and thought. "Let's see. The two older ones are in their twenties now, and the baby, Brian, I guess he's about sixteen."

"Where do they live?"

"Brian's in New York with his mother and stepfather. The last I heard, Danielle was also in New York and Martin was in Miami."

"Oh. They are far away," said Jade.

"Yes.".

Soon, they were pulling into the driveway in front of the retirement community and the limo driver stopped, got out, and opened the doors. As they stepped out, Lexi observed Charlotte looking around the area near the front doors of the building, and looked at Charlotte with a questioning look on her face.

"Are you looking for someone, Charlotte?"

"No. Just being observant."

Charlotte smiled at her and they made their way into the building. As they rode the elevator to the second floor, Jade said, "Well, this elevator's not quite as exciting as the other one was."

Lexi laughed and Charlotte replied, "Well, that's okay. I don't think this old body could stand any more excitement tonight."

Jade looked worried. "Are you okay, Ms. T? Did we do too much?"

"I'm fine, don't worry. Just a little tired."

They entered her apartment and Charlotte switched on some lights. She turned to the girls. "Would you like to watch a little TV before bedtime?"

Jade answered first. "No, thanks. I'm gonna try to finish my book." She picked a book up off the coffee table and settled onto the couch.

"I think I'd better start our laundry, if that's okay, Charlotte," answered Lexi.

"Oh, sure. Just wait here a sec and I'll be right back to help you."

Charlotte turned away and walked into her bedroom, looking around to be sure he wasn't there. She looked in her closet and checked the bathroom. Clear. She walked back into the living area then down the hall to the kitchen. Clear again. Next, she opened the French doors to the balcony and peered out. Nobody on the balcony. She tried to look across the street but it was dark and she couldn't see much of anything. She closed the door, turned, and almost bumped into Lexi.

"Oh!"

"I'm sorry, Charlotte, did I scare you?"

"You just startled me, Lexi."

"Are you looking for something?"

"No. I – well, I just like to check everything out when I first get home. It's silly, I know. I just want to be sure we're safe, that's all."

"Oh. Are you afraid Dennis might come by here?"

"Who?"

"You know, the guy I told you about. With the black pickup truck."

"Oh. Yes. Well, we can't be too cautious, can we?"

"Charlotte, I'm sorry if our being here is scary for you. Maybe we shouldn't stay here."

"Oh, no! Your being here doesn't scare me. I feel better, having you here. Now come on, let's get started with the laundry. Let's find a t-shirt of mine that Jade can wear to sleep in, so she can change and you can wash her clothes."

A little later, Jade was asleep in Charlotte's bed, the clothes were in the drier, and Lexi and Charlotte were sitting at the kitchen table, drinking hot tea.

"Charlotte, thank you so much for everything you did for us tonight. I'll bet I had the best graduation celebration of anyone at my school."

"You're welcome. I enjoyed it, too. It's nice to have someone to spoil a little."

"So, what's up with your family?"

"What do you mean?"

Lexi shrugged. "I don't know. It seems like you're all spread out, all over the place, and you don't even see your grandkids. Is that intentional?"

"Intentional. Hmm. I'm not sure how to answer that question. Maybe it's partly intentional, yes."

"But why? Don't you like them?"

"I think it's more that they don't like me, Lexi. But really, it's just that we've been apart so long, we're practically strangers."

"How could they not like you, Charlotte? I don't see how that could be true."

"Oh, Lexi. The truth is, I don't know how they could like me, even a little. I've done some horrible things in my life, Lexi. I haven't always been the "sweet old lady" you see before you now."

Lexi took a sip of tea. "You told me earlier that you were giving me the short version of the story surrounding your name. So, how about you give me the long version now?"

Charlotte considered her question. She knew if she was honest with Lexi, she risked losing her and Jade already. She didn't know if she could face another loss. In a short time, they'd become important to her. Silly, she knew. But she wasn't just thinking about her own feelings. Honestly, she was afraid for them. She was hoping she could keep them safe. But that was ridiculous. How could she keep them safe? She couldn't even keep herself safe.

Charlotte sighed. What would Lexi think of her if she told her the truth?

"Charlotte? How about it?"

"Okay. But I'm going to need a glass of wine for this."

Lexi shook her head. "Really? You *need* a glass of wine?"

"Okay. No wine. But let's move to the living room, where it's a little more comfortable."

As she walked by the bedroom door, Charlotte peeked inside. Jade was sound asleep. She closed the door and headed toward her living room chair. Lexi sprawled out on the couch.

"By the way, Charlotte, I really didn't want us to kick you out of your bedroom. I feel bad that you'll be sleeping on the couch."

"Oh, don't worry about it. Actually, I often sleep on the couch, so it's no big deal."

"Well, anyway, thanks. It's nice of you to let us stay here tonight. Now, tell me what's going on with you."

"I'm not sure where to start."

"How about the beginning?"

The beginning. Oh, dear.

Chapter 23

Charlotte closed her eyes and thought back over the past fifty or so years. As always, her thoughts first turned to Marty, and she smiled. She decided to tell her about Marty; a safe place to begin. She opened her eyes and looked over at Lexi.

"When I was about your age, I met the love of my life, Marty Sanderson."

Lexi smiled. "How'd you meet him?"

"At a dance hall in Tulsa. I grew up in a small town in Oklahoma. My girlfriends and I used to go to this dance hall every Friday night and on this one night, I was getting a coke at the concession stand, and he was working there. When he handed my drink to me, our fingers brushed and I swear, it was like an electrical shock went through me. I looked at him and he smiled. He was so handsome! He told me he'd get a break in twenty minutes and hoped I would dance with him. He later told me he'd had the same sensation when we touched," she laughed.

"Probably static electricity or something, but we both took it to mean so much more. Anyway, after that night, we were inseparable. He was a wonderful man, Lexi. Kind, generous, funny, smart. Even my parents loved him, which is saying a lot, because they were difficult to please. He actually worked at a local bank and was saving money for college. He'd been working the concession stand as a volunteer for the Lions Club. Three months after we met, we were engaged. Our wedding was small, but beautiful. Six months after we married, he was drafted."

"Viet Nam?" asked Lexi.

Charlotte nodded. After all these years, her eyes still misted when she spoke of what happened next.

"I was so scared when he was drafted but he assured me everything would be alright. He told me to look at the positive side; he'd do his year in 'Nam, then he'd be able to come back and go to college on the G.I. Bill. But a week after he arrived in Viet Nam, he was killed."

"Oh, no!" exclaimed Lexi. "Charlotte, that's so sad! I'm sorry."

"Thank you. It was incomprehensible to me. Marty was so full of life and had so many dreams for the future. I know he would've done marvelous things with his life, Lexi. It was just so – I don't know – senseless. And on a personal level, I was devastated, of course."

"I can imagine. Is that when you started drinking?"

She considered Lexi's question. Marty's death wasn't exactly what led to the drinking, but did she want to tell Lexi the whole truth? It was such a dark story and Lexi was so young. Lexi had enough burdens of her own. So, once again, Charlotte dodged the truth.

"Not immediately. I guess it wasn't long after that, though."

Though she wouldn't tell Lexi what had happened, she couldn't stop her thoughts from drifting to that horrible night that changed her life. Her parents and friends were all at a loss as to how to help her. She was so depressed and so lost. Carla was especially worried about her friend.

At the time, Carla was a college freshman and had been dating a guy from back east, whom she'd met through some college friends. Douglas was older, out of college and very worldly. Carla seemed infatuated with him. He had come to Oklahoma that weekend to visit Carla and meet her parents.

Anyway, she had told Charlotte that she and Douglas thought it would do her good to get out of the house and go out with them. So, on that fateful Friday night, they went to a college party where Douglas started mixing drinks for the three of them. Charlotte discovered she liked the Tom Collins he offered her; the drink tasted good, but more importantly, she loved how it made her feel – or not feel. So, she drank several more. At first, she just felt warm and happy but it didn't take long before she became a sorry, sad drunk. She started crying and made a bit of a scene.

So, gallant Douglas offered to take her home. He left Carla with a group of their friends, told her he'd get Charlotte home safely and would be right back, not to worry about her. Well, he got her home, alright. But not safely. She passed out in the car and he carried her into her house. She woke up half naked, with him on top of her, raping her. Charlotte recalled how she had tried to scream but he'd covered her mouth with his hand and told her he'd hurt her even worse if she didn't keep quiet. When he was finished, he got up, smiled at her and spoke of how he knew she would never want to hurt Carla by telling her what had happened. After all, it would kill her to know that her slutty girlfriend had seduced her fiancé. He pulled a small box out of his pocket and showed her the ring inside, laughing. He left her, went back to the nightclub, and later that night, proposed to Carla. She accepted.

Lexi interrupted Charlotte's thoughts. "Charlotte. Hello? What happened next?"

"Next? Let's see. Shortly after Marty's death, I learned I was pregnant."

"Well, that was a good thing, right?"

She nodded in agreement. It had been. Sort of. What she couldn't tell Lexi – or anyone else, for that matter – is that she didn't know for sure if the baby was Marty's or the result of the rape. She spent the entire pregnancy in an anxious state, calculating the weeks, wondering if she could love this baby if she thought Douglas was the father. As soon as John was born and she held him, though, she knew in her heart that he was Marty's. Over the years, whenever any doubt would crop up in her mind, she'd consider secretly testing John's DNA but she really didn't know how to do that, without the father's DNA as a comparison. And she wasn't willing to let anyone in on her horrible secret. Plus, as John grew older, he looked more and more like Marty. He even shared some mannerisms with Marty, and eventually she quit considering that Marty may not be his father. And honestly, she was a little afraid to learn the truth; what if Marty wasn't John's father? Would she still love her son as much?

"Yes, Lexi, it was a good thing. I felt like a piece of Marty would live on, you know? And I'd be less lonely. But it was also very

111

difficult. John was a colicky baby and didn't sleep much. I was working and my mother was helping take care of John, but it was still hard. I was young and all of my friends were still out having a good time. Some were in college. And I was home every night, walking the floor with a crying baby. I started to feel very sorry for myself.

It wasn't long before I met another man. He seemed like a life-saver to me. He was very different from Marty. Very loud and boister-ous and had a lot of money. He loved to spend money on me. My parents didn't like him at all and called him Slick Willy." She smiled. "His name was William. Regardless of my parents' feelings – or maybe because of them – I married Slick Willy. At first, we had a lot of fun. We both partied hard. William could afford baby sitters so John was left at home with a sitter quite often. Over the years, we both had af-fairs with other people but by then we had two more children – so, we convinced ourselves it was best to stay together 'for the children.' What a mistake that was. It all came to a head one night in 1983 – fourteen years into the marriage."

"What happened?"

She looked at Lexi. "I can imagine what you must be thinking of me, Lexi. Jumping into that marriage, the drinking, the affairs, leav-ing the children at home while we partied. I wasn't a good person at all, was I?"

Lexi shrugged. "You probably were just doing the best you could at the time."

"That's very generous of you. I wasn't doing my best at all. I wasn't even trying. Anyway, one night, I was at one of John's basketball games. William had stayed home with the girls. One of the other boys' father was sitting near me and we started flirting and talking. Before long, we ended up in the back seat of his car, having sex. And that's how John and this man's son found us, along with most of the basket-ball team and the coach."

"Oh my god!"

She dropped her head. "Yeah. Well, as you can imagine, it was horrible for John. He didn't want to go back to school. Hell, it was

112

hard for the girls, too. This was a small town, so of course, everyone knew about it by the next morning. That sealed the deal, so to speak. William left, I packed up the kids and a few belongings, and moved here to Houston. I had a friend from high school who lived here and she let us stay with her until I could find a job and a place for us to live."

"I'll bet that was hard, moving from a little town in Oklahoma to Houston."

"Actually, it was wonderful. No more small-town gossip. Nobody knew me. It was a fresh start. I didn't have any education beyond high school, though, so any jobs I had didn't pay much. There were times I was working two, even three jobs, just to make ends meet. William paid child support, but that didn't go very far."

"Were you still drinking a lot?"

"I wouldn't say a lot, but when I did, it sure wasn't healthy. I drank when I was sad or overwhelmed, just to feel better. Usually, late at night, by myself, after the kids were in bed. I sure couldn't afford to go out and party, or pay for sitters anymore."

Lexi nodded. "So, this was the eighties. That's still a long time ago. What next?"

"Let's see. Well, I doubt this will shock you, but another man entered my life."

Lexi smiled. "Yeah, I'm not shocked. You didn't like to be without a man, did you?"

Charlotte laughed. "I don't know. Honestly, I didn't put much thought into anything. I was living day-to-day."

"How'd you meet this one?"

"He was Julie's Biology teacher."

"You're kidding."

"No. He was a very nice man. Michael San Angelo. He was everything William wasn't. Studious, quiet, kind, humble. He was a good husband and a wonderful father to my children. They were pretty wary of him at first – can you blame them? But they grew to love him and we made a nice family. That was a good time." Charlotte smiled.

"So, what happened to Michael? Did you end up divorced?"

"No. He died of a heart attack in 1990. He was handing out tests to his class and just dropped dead. It was totally unexpected."

"How awful! So, you were a widow again."

"Yes."

"How old were your children?"

"Let's see. When Michael died, John would have been twenty-three, Julie twenty, and Heather fourteen."

"So, was Heather the only one still at home?"

"Yes. John had graduated from college and was working at a bank. Julie was in college in Boulder, Colorado. Heather was a freshman in high school."

"And the drinking?"

"At first, it was bad. I was so angry."

"Angry?"

"Yes. At God. At the world. At Michael for leaving me."

"Really?"

"I know. It sure didn't make sense to be angry at Michael. But as you've noted, I didn't do "alone" very well. My marriage to Michael hadn't been a great love affair, but it had been good – I mean, he was sweet to me and the kids, he provided us with a nice home, and he loved me dearly. And now he was gone."

"Did you love him?"

"Oh, sure. I did love him. It wasn't the same as the love I'd had for Marty, but then, I wasn't a young, eighteen-year-old with all these romantic notions I'd had back then. My life with Michael had been – I don't know – safe and secure, comfortable, happy. And now I'd lost that. I didn't know what to do with myself. So, I reverted to old habits and started drinking again."

Lexi shook her head. "I can't believe you were like that, Charlotte. You seem so together now."

"Well, it took me an awfully long time to grow up, Lexi. I'm sure you're much more mature at eighteen than I was in my forties."

"So, what did Heather think about your drinking?"

"At first, she didn't say much. But then she started hiding my liquor. It drove me crazy. Then one Sunday afternoon, she brought one of her teachers to the house to speak with me."

"Did you know the teacher?"

"Sort of. He was a history teacher and had been a friend of Michael's. They didn't teach at the same school, but they knew each other through a teachers' softball league. Anyway, he was a recovering alcoholic and he sat me down and spoke with me about it. At first, I denied having a problem. But he convinced me to go to AA meetings with him. I did slip a couple of times, but I eventually sobered up and stayed sober for years. My life greatly improved without alcohol."

"In what ways?"

"First and foremost, I started thinking about other people more than myself. I became a better mother. As I continued attending meetings, I became better at selecting the people I associated with, and started thinking more about the consequences of my actions. I quit feeling sorry for myself. Eventually, I started taking some college classes at night.

I graduated from The University of Houston with a Bachelor of Arts in Humanities in 1997. Heather and I actually attended school together for a while! Anyway, I began working for the Jung Center and also started writing. Honestly, Lexi, I think writing saved my life."

"In what way?"

"It was better than therapy. It helped me sort out my feelings and express myself in a non-threatening way. And I learned that other people who read my work, shared many of the same experiences and feelings as me. It helped me connect with people. And it didn't hurt that I found some success with it, which helped with my level of self-confidence. I was also doing quite well, financially, which relieved a lot of stress in my life. Finally, I was self-reliant. I wasn't depending on a man to support me, financially or otherwise."

"So, you were finally happy?"

She nodded. "Very happy."

"What about your kids? What happened to all of them?"

"Well, John had a very successful career in banking. He and his first wife had three children – the grandchildren I told you and Jade about. They divorced a few years ago, and John met his current wife, Marlene. I'm not too crazy about her – I feel like she's only interested in John's money. But who am I to judge, right? Anyway, he retired early last year and they moved to Florida. They have a condo on the beach in Panama City, which I'm sure his children love to visit. He's a good man, especially considering how he was raised. Our relationship has been a little rocky, as you can imagine. But for a long time, he was the only child I had nearby, since he and I both lived in Houston and the girls moved away. So, he was the one stuck with making sure I was okay."

"I doubt he looked at it that way."

"Oh, I don't know. But even if he didn't enjoy it, he's always been very responsible when it comes to his old mother. It's more than I deserve from him, that's for sure."

"And the girls?"

"Julie, my middle child, lives in Denver. She's never married and has no children. She's a very successful business owner. She quit college after her freshman year, but she stayed in Colorado and she and a friend co-own a tea shop in downtown Denver. She lives in an apartment above the shop."

"Does the friend live with her?"

"Oh, no. The friend is a man, and he lives with his wife and children in the suburbs somewhere."

"Do you have a good relationship with Julie?"

"Not so much. Of the three, she probably suffered the most from my mistakes, due to her age. I mean, we don't fight or anything, but she's just, well, distant I guess. She doesn't share much about her life with me and I don't see her very often. She says she can't get away because of the business, and I don't press the issue. I think she's happy, though."

"And Heather? She's the youngest?"

116

"Yes. Heather's my baby. She and I have a very good relationship. She lives in California with her wife, Ariana."

"Wife? She's gay?"

"Yes."

"Does that bother you?"

"Not at all. I've known Heather was gay since she was sixteen, and even then, it didn't come as a surprise. She and Ariana are great together. They've been together about five years and were married about a month before my stroke. Heather produces documentaries and Ariana is a civil rights attorney. They have two little Yorkshire Terriers that are adorable. I see them fairly often. In fact, they may come for a visit soon. I hope so, anyway. They're both very busy people, so it's not always easy for them to get away."

"They have cool jobs."

"Yes. They do."

"So, why did you start drinking again, Charlotte? Was it the stroke? And what is this big secret you have now?"

"Big secret?"

"I think it has something to do with the man who paid for our dinner tonight. Come on. I'm not stupid. I know something is up. Tell me about it."

Chapter 24

Lexi was right; she's not stupid. How much could she tell her?

"Charlotte?"

She sighed. "Okay. You're right. There's more to the story. I'll be honest with you, though – I can't tell you everything. But I'll tell you as much as I can."

She nodded. "Okay."

"A little before the night of my stroke, I started receiving messages from someone."

"Messages?"

"Text messages. Phone calls. I stopped answering the calls and he'd leave voice mail messages."

"Did you know who the calls were from, Charlotte?"

"Oh, yes. I knew."

"And the calls were threatening in some way?"

"Oh, not overtly. The threats were subtle. If you read them, or heard them, you might not know they were threats. But I knew."

"What did you do about it?"

"Nothing, really. I tried to ignore them. But the calls brought up a lot of terrible memories, Lexi. I was frightened, yes. But more than that, I was – ashamed."

"Ashamed?"

"Yes. I've told you enough about my life tonight for you to know I have a lot to be ashamed about, right? And I didn't tell you everything. Anyway, I was a wreck. I saw an ad for this senior citizen trip to the casinos in Louisiana. At first, my thought was that it would be a good way just to get away and have some fun, you know? But I was kidding myself. I knew I'd drink. And I did."

"So, what happened?"

"Until the stroke, it really wasn't terrible. I played the machines and lost a little money. I had several rum and cokes while I was gambling. Then I had something to eat. But before I could even get on the bus to come home, I had the stroke."

"Do you think the threatening messages you'd been receiving caused your stroke?"

"Oh, I doubt it. The stroke was probably due to years of abusing my body with very unhealthy habits, not to mention heredity. My father died after having a stroke, and my mother had two heart attacks before she died. I guess it's possible that the stress may have contributed to my stroke, but who knows? Anyway, when I got back to Houston, John had arranged for me to live here. At first, I lived in the area where they provide more care because I couldn't take care of myself. John put my condo up for sale and when I was able to live on my own again, he arranged for the apartment and had some of my things moved here. "

"Is that what you wanted? Or did he do all of that without your permission?"

"Oh, I agreed to it. I wouldn't say it was what I wanted, but I really had no choice. I was pretty helpless for a while there."

"You seem to be doing really well now, Charlotte."

"Yes, I think so, too." She smiled.

"And the guy at the restaurant tonight? Was that the guy who made the threats?"

"Well, I didn't see him so I can't say for sure. But probably."

"Who is he?"

"My best friend's husband."

"What?!"

"Yes. My friend, Carla – her husband, Douglas. He's a horrible man. And he doesn't care for me. Carla died recently, and the calls and text messages started soon after that. His daughter, Debra, called me a few days ago to tell me he's in Houston. Apparently, Carla made some investments and left me some money. He found out about it, and he's angry."

"Wow. That's crazy. Didn't she leave him any money?"

Charlotte laughed. "I have no idea, but he doesn't need any more money, Lexi. The man is a millionaire, several times over. Maybe a billionaire, I don't know. His family was very prominent in Philadelphia, very wealthy. He continued in the family business and has more money than anyone could ever spend."

"So, why does he care that she left you some money?"

Charlotte shrugged. "It doesn't make sense, does it? But as I said, he's a horrible man. He was always very controlling of Carla, and I'm sure it drives him crazy to know she had made those investments without his knowledge. Then, to top it off, she left it to me, a woman he hated. A woman who hated him."

"He sounds awful. Why did Carla stay married to him?"

"I don't know, Lexi. I wish she'd never married him in the first place. When we were young, Carla was so happy and full of life. Very outgoing. She loved to go out dancing and spending time with friends. But over the years, he beat her down. She became very insecure."

"Did you spend a lot of time with her?"

"Not really. They moved back east, to Philadelphia. She and I would take vacations together sometimes. She'd send me a ticket to meet her somewhere, and always paid for the hotel rooms and meals. We always had fun together."

"I'm surprised that Douglas guy let her do that."

"Me, too. I'm sure she paid for it."

"You mean, he'd treat her badly after the trips?"

"Probably. She never let on, though. But she said enough for me to know she wasn't happy with him. And then, I also received a letter from her around the time of her death, which confirmed that."

"That's so sad."

"Yes, it is."

"So, what are you going to do now?"

"That's what I need to figure out, Lexi. Debra wants me to come to Santa Fe, to deal with the paperwork surrounding the money Carla left me. So, I guess I need to try to do that. But that's not the only thing concerning me right now."

120

"What else is there?"

"You and Jade."

"Me and Jade? Why?"

"Lexi, I'm very worried about you two. This Dennis character means you harm, your mother's in jail. You can't keep working and looking after Jade, all by yourself. I want to help you."

"Charlotte, it's not your problem. I'll figure it out."

"Well, I know you're very capable. But it doesn't hurt to accept a little help from friends, either. So, I'm working on a plan."

"A plan?"

"Yes. But it's late, Lexi. I think it's time we both get some sleep. We can talk more tomorrow. You get off at three tomorrow, right?"

"Yes, ma'am. I'll come by and get Jade and we'll get out of your hair. I work a half day on Saturday, then in the afternoon, we're going to get groceries then go to the county jail to visit Regina."

"You have a busy weekend ahead of you."

"Yeah, I guess. But I'm off on Sunday. Other than a little housework, Jade and I can just chill all day."

"Good. You deserve a break."

"Well, I'd better get to bed, Charlotte. Would you like some help making your bed on the couch?"

"No, I'll be fine. I do need to go change into my PJ's, though. I'll just be a moment."

"Okay."

Charlotte made her way through the bedroom and into the bathroom, got ready for bed, and returned to the living room a few minutes later. Lexi stood and walked toward the bedroom. She turned as she reached the door, and thanked Charlotte again for the graduation celebration.

"You're welcome, Lexi. I'm glad you enjoyed it. Good night."

"Good night, Charlotte."

Chapter 25

After the bedroom door closed, Charlotte fished her phone out of her handbag and checked for messages. Of course. There it was; a text message from him.

I hope you enjoyed your dinner, Charlotte. I must say, I'm disappointed that you haven't changed your lying ways...Denver, huh? It's time you and I had a little talk. I look forward to seeing you soon.

So, no doubt now that it was him at the restaurant. He'd managed to follow them without her being aware of his presence, which was very unnerving. She looked over at the front door to ensure the deadbolt was turned and the security chain was in place. She kept the table lamp on and settled onto the couch with a throw pillow and quilt. She tried to sleep but had way too much on her mind. Finally, after tossing and turning for a couple of hours, she gave up and walked back to the kitchen. She made herself a cup of tea, then came back to the living room and considered her options.

She used her cell phone to access the web site of Jade's school. There was an announcement about the assembly, which started at ten o'clock. She sent an e-mail to the front desk downstairs, asking about getting a ride on the van in the morning. She felt the van would be safer than riding alone in a public cab. After the assembly, she'd have to rely on a cab or the bus, since Jade would be with her, but that couldn't be helped. She looked over at the clock on the mantel – 1:30. Damn. She really needed to try and sleep. She settled back on the couch and eventually managed to sleep a little, off and on. When she opened her eyes at five-thirty, she could hear the shower running. She sat up, folded the quilt and went to the kitchen to make coffee. She peered out the French door blinds; it was raining.

Well, I can make a nice, hot breakfast for the girls, she decided. She set about making scrambled eggs and toast and sliced some strawberries. She heard the bedroom door open and Lexi came out wearing her work uniform, hair still wet from the shower.

"Morning, Charlotte."

"Good morning, Lexi. Is Jade up yet?"

"No, I'll let her sleep a little longer. She doesn't take long to get ready, and since she can catch the bus right down the street, she won't need a lot of time to get to school."

"The coffee's ready. You and I can go ahead and eat breakfast now, before it gets cold. I'll make some more for Jade when she gets up."

"Oh! No, you shouldn't do that. I'll just wake her up now."

"Lexi, it's okay. Get your coffee and I'll put the food on the table."

"Are you sure?"

"Of course. Please. Sit."

"Well, if you're sure…" she helped herself to coffee, added vanilla cream to it, and sat down. Charlotte set her plate in front of her and sat down across from her.

"This looks great, Charlotte. Thanks."

Charlotte just smiled and started eating.

"So, what is the plan you mentioned last night, Charlotte?"

Charlotte took a swig of coffee and looked over at her. "I think I need to go to Santa Fe."

"To meet with Debra."

"Yes. But I don't want to try and make the trip alone. Now, if you don't like this idea, please be honest with me, but what do you think of coming with me?"

Lexi frowned. "To Santa Fe?"

"Yes."

"I don't know. I mean, sure, I'd like to go. But I just don't see how I could. I mean, there's Jade, my job, Regina. It would be complicated, that's for sure."

"I know. But Jade would come, too. Of course, we'd need your mother's permission. I could go to the jail with you tomorrow to visit her. Do you know yet how long she'll be there?"

"Not really. They're keeping her there until she has her probation hearing. Her lawyer told her she'll probably get revoked and go back to prison for two or three years. But it could be a while before she has the hearing and gets moved out of the county."

"Any chance her probation won't be revoked?"

"I doubt it. She's already had her share of second chances."

"Well, I have a friend who works for the family courts. I met her when I was doing research for one of my books. I plan to call her today to ask her about your legal rights surrounding Jade. You know — can you be her guardian? If not, what would I need to do to be her guardian? Unless, of course, there are other family members, such as Jade's father."

"You're kidding, right?"

"About her father?"

"No. Well, that too, yes. But I meant about you becoming her guardian. Why would you want to do that?"

"To keep her out of the foster care system. Don't get me wrong, I know there are some really good people out there, foster parents who are loving and caring. But there are also some bad situations. I don't feel comfortable playing Russian roulette with Jade's life. I told you I did some research for a recent book; it included a lot of research on foster care in Texas. I also remember you saying that you and Jade had experience with foster care and didn't want to do that again.

Look, I know I'm far from perfect, but I think I can provide a good home for the two of you, at least until your mother is out of prison and on her feet. I would like to do that, whether you're Jade's guardian or I am. Of course, you and Jade would need to agree; I wouldn't want to do this if you didn't want me to. I also need to straighten out the situation with Douglas White, and also with that Dennis character, so we'll all be safe."

Lexi's eyes teared up and her lip trembled.

"Oh my, I've upset you. I'm sorry. We don't have to pursue this plan, if you don't want to." Charlotte reached over and grabbed her hand. "Don't be upset."

Lexi smiled at her. "I'm not upset, Charlotte. I'm just so – in awe. I can't believe how nice you're being to us."

"So, you like the plan?"

"Yes, but I want to wait until after you've talked with your friend, before I mention it to Jade. I don't want to get her hopes up, if we can't do this."

"That's a good idea."

"And another thing, Charlotte."

"Yes?"

Lexi looked as if she was afraid to say it, but she did – "No drinking, Charlotte."

"I know."

"I mean it. I mean, what you're offering to do for us is very generous and you probably think I have no right to even bring this up. But Jade's been through enough. I don't want her to go from having to deal with an addict to having to deal with an alcoholic."

"You're right. No drinking. It won't be a problem. I promise."

"Can you really make that promise, Charlotte?"

She stared at Lexi, then looked down and thought about her question. She sighed. "You're right. I can't guarantee anything. But I feel confident about this, Lexi. I do promise to give it my best shot."

Lexi considered that response for a moment. "Okay. But you can't have kids stay with you here, right?"

"That's right. No more than two weeks at a time. But that's not a problem. We can move into my condo. I've already taken it off the market, anyway."

"Where's your condo?"

"Not far from here."

"And the Santa Fe trip, well, how long would we be gone? I mean, I have this job."

"I know. I'd be happy to speak with the director here, and explain to her that I need you to drive me, and ask that she give you some time off. I'll also pay you for your time, so you won't suffer the loss of your paycheck. I'm thinking no more than a week, probably less. I'll also cover all of your expenses, meals, all that, so it won't cost you anything. We'll also manage to have some fun along the way – make a little vacation out of it, you know?"

Lexi shook her head. "You are too good to be true, Charlotte."

"Not really. I've had some hard times in my life, and I know how much it can help to have a little support from someone during the hard times. I'm just "paying it forward," as they say. So, if Regina okays it, and the information I get from my friend is helpful, are you up for a road trip?"

"What road trip?" They turned and saw Jade rubbing her eyes and walking toward the kitchen.

"Well, hello, sleepy head. I was just talking with your sister about a trip I may take to Santa Fe to visit a friend's daughter. Did you sleep well?"

She nodded.

"Are you hungry?"

"A little."

"Well, have a seat and I'll get your breakfast. How about a mug of hot chocolate?"

"Yes, please."

So, she got up and fixed breakfast for Jade while Lexi went and dried her hair. After Jade finished eating, she got dressed and within a short time, the girls were heading out the door.

"Are you going to watch us from the balcony, Ms. T?" asked Jade.

"Jade, no, it's raining," said Lexi.

"Oh, sorry. I forgot about that."

"I'll tell you what. I'll open the blinds and watch through the windows. You should be able to see me wave at you. And then I'll be at your school for the assembly at ten, so be sure to look for me there, okay?"

Jade ran back to her and gave her a hug. "Thank you, Charlotte."

She squeezed her tight. "I can't wait to see you get an award!"

126

The girls left and she walked back to the kitchen. She opened the blinds on the French doors and watched for them out the window panes of the doors. Soon, she spotted them crossing the street, using an umbrella she'd loaned them. They walked down toward the bus stop and stood waiting for the bus. As Jade got on the bus, she turned and waved and Charlotte waved back at her. Lexi held the umbrella and looked up at her. After the bus pulled away, she watched as Lexi walked back toward the building. Thankfully, there was no sign of Dennis or his truck.

Chapter 26

Luckily, she was able to secure a ride on the van and soon, was on her way to Jade's school and enjoying a chat with Jerry, the driver. It was still raining and according to the news reports, there was a risk of flash flooding. As they neared the school, Jerry asked about a pick-up time.

"Well, I don't think I can use the van to return home, Jerry. I'll have Jade with me, so we'll probably get a cab. I know the van is only for residents."

Jerry frowned. "Any idea how long this awards ceremony will last?"

"I'm not sure, but I don't think very long."

"These things at my kids' schools usually take less than an hour. Then sometimes, you find yourself visiting with teachers and other parents. How about this, Ms. Tilian? When the assembly is over, you send me a text." He grabbed a piece of paper off a sticky notepad on his dashboard. "Here's the number. I'll take my lunch break and come and get you in my own car. How's that sound?"

"Oh. Well, are you sure you don't mind doing that?"

"Of course, I don't mind. I wouldn't want someone leaving my mom stranded, and I'm not gonna do that to you."

He pulled into the school parking lot and found a vacant hand-icapped spot not too far from the front doors. He started to get out of the van but she stopped him. "Jerry, don't get out and get wet, it's not necessary. I can open my own door without your help. Thank you for the ride and I'll see you soon."

He started to protest but she was already opening the passen-ger door and stepping out. She shut the door, waved up at him, and opened her umbrella. She only had a few feet to walk, anyway, before reaching the covered walkway. Jerry waited and watched her until she reached the front door of the school, then pulled out and left. She shook out the umbrella and made her way to the office to check in, as

Lexi had instructed. Before long, she was sitting in the cafeteria/auditorium, along with a lot of parents and small children. Then the students entered the cafeteria, walking in a line two abreast, and sat in chairs marked "Reserved." The teachers sat in a row on the stage, facing the audience. A short, grey-haired woman walked to the podium and switched on a microphone.

"Can everyone hear me?"

They all answered in the affirmative and she smiled and welcomed everyone to this year's awards ceremony. A student then led them in the pledge of allegiance and the Texas pledge, followed by two songs from the school choir. The distribution of awards then began, with children receiving awards for academics and attendance. Charlotte looked over at the area where the students were sitting and searched for Jade. She spotted her and it appeared she was also looking for someone. Finally, their eyes met and Jade smiled and waved. She waved back. Jade poked the little girl sitting next to her and said something to her. The girl looked back toward Charlotte, as Jade pointed and whispered. Charlotte waved and the girl smiled at her. She wondered what Jade had told her friend about her. Did she say she was a friend? A grandparent?

Then Jade's name was announced; she was receiving a perfect attendance award. Charlotte clapped loudly. She found it incredible that this child, with the circumstances she faced at home, had managed to miss not one day of school. What an accomplishment! Jade received her little trophy and turned toward her and held it up, pumping her fist in the air as in victory, with her other hand. Several parents chuckled but Charlotte held up her arm and pumped her fist in return at Jade. The smile on her little face was priceless.

She was even prouder of her little friend, Jade, when a short time later she received the first-place award for Art Achievement. She couldn't help herself – she stood up and clapped and cheered. Charlotte may have even managed to embarrass Jade, but she didn't care. She was so proud of her. As she sat back down, a woman sitting next to her asked, "Is that your granddaughter?" She didn't hesitate at all as she answered, "Yes. My youngest grandchild."

"She's beautiful."

She nodded. "Yes, she is."

After the ceremony, the place got a little crazy, with children running around and saying goodbye to each other, parents speaking with teachers, and the younger siblings of students running around or crying. She pulled out her phone and sent a text to Jerry then started to look for Jade. Before long, Jade found her and ran up and hugged her. She pulled back and held up her trophies. "Look, Ms. T, they even have my name on them!"

"Wow, that's really something! Congratulations, Jade."

"Thank you. Do you want to meet my art teacher?"

"Of course!"

She grabbed her hand and led Charlotte toward the front of the room, where the art teacher was talking with a group of students. She seemed to be a very popular teacher. As they approached her, Charlotte realized she knew her. Years ago, she'd been the art teacher at the school where Michael had taught. Like Charlotte, she'd aged quite a bit since then, but Charlotte still recognized her.

"Mrs. Washington, I'd like you to meet someone."

Mrs. Washington turned, looked at Jade, then up at Charlotte and looked surprised. "Why, Charlotte! What a surprise! How the heck are you?"

She grabbed Charlotte's hand and Charlotte smiled back at her. "Lorraine. This is a surprise, isn't it? I'm fine."

Jade interrupted. "You two know each other?"

Lorraine nodded. "We sure do. But it's been ages since we've seen each other, hasn't it, Charlotte?" She put her arm around Jade's shoulders and asked, "Aren't you just so proud of our little artist, here? I have to say, I can't remember a student with such a gift. She also works very hard, too. An unbeatable combination."

"Yes, she's pretty amazing," Charlotte answered.

Lorraine Washington turned to Jade. "Now, you have a great summer. I can't wait to see your future work. I'll bet one of these days, your art will be hanging in that fancy museum where your grandmother used to work."

Jade looked at Charlotte sheepishly and didn't correct Lorraine about her not being her grandmother. She simply said, "Thank you, Mrs. Washington. You have a nice summer, too. Enjoy your break from us kids."

Lorraine laughed. "I'll do that, sweetie."

Lorraine turned back to Charlotte. "I hope we see each other again soon. You take care."

"You, too."

Later, as they approached the front doors to leave, Charlotte explained to Jade that Jerry would be picking them up and she didn't know if he'd arrived yet. Luckily, the rain had stopped. They stepped outside and looked around. Then she saw him, walking down the sidewalk toward them. He waved. "Over here, Ms. Tilian!"

He walked up to them and explained that he'd had to park quite a distance from the building, so he'd go back for his car and pull up closer to pick them up. He told them what he was driving then left them to wait for him.

Jade looked up at her. "You aren't mad at me, are you Ms. Tilian?"

"Mad at you? Why on earth would I be mad at you?"

"Well, I let Mrs. Washington think you're my grandma."

"That's okay, I told the lady sitting next to me that you're my granddaughter."

She smiled. "You did?"

"I sure did. It's okay, Jade, it isn't really a lie. I feel like I'm your honorary grandmother. So, it doesn't matter what other people think, does it?"

Jade thought about it. "Lexi says it's bad to lie. She hates lies 'cuz Regina lies so much. But I'll bet even Lexi wouldn't be mad about this, Ms. T."

"I'll bet you're right. But we can ask her about it later, okay?"

"Okay."

As they rode home, Jade and Jerry chattered the entire way about the awards ceremony and his kids. Before long, they were back in Charlotte's apartment and she was preparing some lunch. The doorbell buzzed and Jade ran toward the door.

"Wait, Jade! Don't answer it."

Jade stopped and turned around. "Why not?"

"Let me see who it is first, that's all."

"Yes, ma'am."

Charlotte peeked out the peephole and saw that it was Lexi. "It's okay, it's your sister."

Charlotte opened the door and let Lexi in, then closed and locked the door behind her. Jade ran back to the kitchen for her trophies and shoved them toward Lexi. "Look what I got, Lexi!"

Lexi was appropriately impressed and congratulated her little sister, giving high-fives and saying, "Way to go!" Jade turned to Charlotte and asked, "Can I show her the pictures, Ms. T?"

"Of course. Here you go." She handed her the phone and Jade showed Lexi the photos Charlotte had taken today of Jade with her trophies and some of her friends from school.

"Charlotte, thanks for going today. Jade, I wish I could've been there."

"That's okay, I know you had to work. People thought Ms. T was my grandma, Lexi. And we let them think that; is that okay? I mean, I guess it's a lie, but Ms. T said she feels like she's my – my – what did you call it, Ms. T?"

"Honorary grandmother."

"Yeah. That's it. Honorary grandma. So, does that make it okay? I think it does."

Lexi smiled. "Yeah, you goofball. It's okay."

Jade smiled. "Good. I like having an – whatever it is you called it. Special Grandma."

Charlotte laughed. "Oh, I'm special, alright!"

Lexi also laughed.

"What?" asked Jade, confused.

"Nothing, Jade," replied Lexi. "Don't worry about it."

After lunch, Lexi went back to work and Jade sat in the living room, watching TV while Charlotte went into her bedroom to make some phone calls. She soon had all the information she needed and joined Jade in the living room.

"What are they doing to that house?" Charlotte asked.

"It's Demo Day," she answered.

"Demo Day?"

"Mm hmm. They demolish it, then renovate it." She rewound the show a bit. "See, this is what it used to look like."

"Not too nice."

"Nope. But wait 'til you see what it looks like when they get through with it. It'll be beautiful, you'll see."

"Okay. I can't wait."

They watched the rest of that show, then started another one.

"You know, Jade, this show gives me an idea."

"What's that, Ms. T? You wanna renovate your apartment?"

"Not this apartment, no. But I still own another place. It's bigger than this apartment, but it's older. It could use some demo and reno, as you say. Maybe you and Lexi could even help me with ideas."

Jade got all excited. "Oh, Ms. T! That would be so much fun! Could I do the demo?!"

Charlotte laughed. "Well, I don't know about that. I sure don't want anyone getting hurt and that looks kind of dangerous. But I'm sure there'd be something you could do."

"What style do you like?"

"Style?"

"Yes. You know – modern or classic, open concept, rustic, that sort of thing. What's your style?"

"To be honest, I don't really know."

Jade looked very serious. "Well, then, you need to watch some more shows with me. It will help you figure out what you like."

"That sounds like a good plan."

"So, are you going to move back to your other place? Or are you going to fix it up and sell it?"

"I'm thinking of moving back to it."

"What's it like?"

"Well, it's a condo but it's in a small complex with just a few other condos. It has a nice little patio and garden space with it, and a garage. It has two bedrooms and a smaller room I always used as an office but it could be a bedroom."

"How many bathrooms?"

"Two. The master bath and another full bathroom off the hall-way by the other bedrooms."

"Is it open concept? Are there lots of windows? Is it two-story or one-story?"

"It's sort of open, I guess. The kitchen opens up to the dining room. There's an archway between the living area and the dining room."

"Is it a big dining room?

"Not really. Average sized, I guess. The table I had seats four comfortably but I could always squeeze in a couple more chairs if I needed to. The entire condo is ground level, so no stairs. It really doesn't have a lot of windows. That's one thing I've never liked about it; it's kind of dark. But it's also very secluded and private, which I liked."

"Were your neighbors nice?"

"Oh, yes. Very nice."

"Do they still live there?"

"I think so."

"How long have you been gone?

"Gosh, let me think. Probably about eight months or so."

"And it's been for sale all this time?"

"Well, no. John – that's my son – didn't put it on the market right away. But probably about six months or so. Why?"

"It probably needs some renovation for it to sell, Ms. T. I don't mean to hurt your feelings, but I bet if you fixed it up, it would sell quicker."

"You're probably right, Jade. I lived in that place a long time. I'm sure it could use some freshening up to bring it up to today's standards. Now, I'll just plan on fixing it up with the idea of moving back into it, though."

"After you fix it up, can Lexi and I visit you there sometimes? Do they allow kids?"

"Of course!"

"Good! This will be fun, Ms. T. Maybe it could be a summer project, fixing up your condo."

"I think it sounds like a perfect summer project."

"Wait 'til I tell Regina. She'll be excited."

"Really?"

"Yes, ma'am. Regina's kinda crazy, but she's pretty artsy. I guess that's where I got it from. She likes decorating and stuff. She might even have some good ideas for us."

"Well, we'll definitely have to get her opinions, then."

Jade smiled then frowned. "Yeah. But I bet it'll be a long time before she gets to see your condo, Ms. T. Lexi says she's probably going to prison."

Charlotte nodded. "Yes, she might. But let's not worry about that today, okay? We'll just take things one day at a time."

"Like N.A.?"

"You know about N.A.?"

"Sure. A.A., N.A., Al-Anon. All that stuff. And they say to take things one day at a time, too. I don't really get it, though. I like thinking ahead."

Charlotte laughed. "I know what you mean. I think it just means not to dwell on the past or stress about the future. Just do the best you can, each day."

Jade nodded. "That's a good way to look at it."

"I agree."

Chapter 27

A little past three, Lexi came back to the apartment to pick up Jade. Before they left, Charlotte told Lexi she had planned to take her to the DMV today to take her driving test, but with all the rain they'd had, many of the streets were impassable and she really didn't think it was safe to try to do that today.

"You're right. I'd be pretty nervous, too, trying to drive on these wet roads. But thanks for thinking about it."

"No problem. After all, that's been the purpose of the driving lessons."

Lexi nodded. "Yes, ma'am. But I have a feeling you won't need me to drive you around much longer. You can probably drive yourself, now."

"Yes, but I need to get an okay from my doctor first. There are a lot of things to consider, besides the use of my hands and feet."

"Such as?"

"Reaction time. Clear thinking and processing of information. Vision. I don't want to drive if I could put other people at risk."

"I see. I hadn't thought about that, Charlotte. Anyway, I don't mind driving you around, as long as you need me to. Except, of course, when you wanna ride in a limo!"

Charlotte laughed. "That doesn't happen often, Lexi. So, tomorrow, what time do you plan to go to the jail?"

"Probably around four."

"I'd like to go with you."

Jade spoke up. "Ms. T is gonna renovate her condo, Lexi. I told her Regina might have some ideas."

Lexi looked at Charlotte knowingly, as she knew Charlotte wanted to speak with Regina about taking them to Santa Fe, and maybe even guardianship but she didn't want to say anything to Jade about it yet.

"Oh, Lexi. I spoke to the friend I talked with you about earlier," said Charlotte. "She had good news for me."

"What kind of news?" asked Jade.

"Never mind, Jade. Ms. Charlotte can tell you about it later. We need to go. Grab your stuff."

"Okay, okay."

Jade put her trophies in her backpack and the two of them left. As they walked out, Lexi looked over her shoulder at Charlotte and mouthed "thank you" silently. Charlotte just smiled and as she locked the front door behind them, her cell phone buzzed. She picked up the phone. Of course, it was him. She ignored the call and set the phone down on the coffee table. She went to the balcony and watched the girls until the bus came, they got on, and it pulled away. She then went back into the apartment and to her desk to check her e-mail. She'd received the anticipated message, containing the documents she'd need Regina to sign. She sure hoped she'd let the girls go to Santa Fe with her. If not, it would mean flying to Albuquerque, then riding in a shuttle to Santa Fe. She really didn't want to navigate airports yet. It would probably require getting assistance from airline employees and using a wheelchair. She hated feeling like an invalid and air travel just wore her out, anyway. Plus, the trip to Santa Fe would be a good experience for the girls. Well, no point in worrying about it today. She'd find out soon enough if they'd be able to make the trip together.

She heard the alert on her phone, indicating she'd received a text message. She returned to the living room, picked up the phone, and read the message:

I hope you like your surprise.

What on earth?

Just then, the doorbell buzzed. Warily, she made her way to the front door and looked out. It was Peter, holding a plant.

Charlotte opened the door. "Hello, Peter."

"Good afternoon, Ms. Tilian. This plant just arrived for you. Where would you like it?"

He stepped in and she motioned toward the living room. "Anywhere is fine, Peter. Thank you."

He set the plant down on the coffee table and as he stepped back out, said "Have a good evening, Ms. Tilian. Oh, and by the way, I haven't seen that gentleman again."

"That's good. Thank you, Peter."

She shut the door, locked up, and walked over to the plant. She pulled the card out of the attached envelope and read: "Can't wait to see you again."

No name. But of course, she knew who had sent the plant. She picked it up, went back to the kitchen, and dropped the plant in the garbage can. The phone dinged again, indicating another text. Sighing, she picked up the phone and read the message.

Do you like it?

She put the phone back down, sat on the couch, and picked up the TV remote. She'd just watch some TV and try to forget about him. A few minutes later, she had another text.

Take a little peek outside. I have another surprise for you.

Oh, my god. This was getting really creepy. She couldn't help herself; she got up and walked back to the French doors. She peeked out the blinds and looked outside. There he was. Standing across the street, on the sidewalk, looking up toward her balcony. He smiled and waved and she dropped the blind. Shit! She walked back to the front of the apartment and made sure the door was secure. She considered calling 911 but what would she say? Douglas White, famous millionaire and philanthropist had sent her a plant? She considered her options. She was probably as safe here as anywhere. If she were to leave the apartment, he'd just follow her and then she'd be more vulnerable. So, she'd just sit tight. He couldn't stand out there across the street all night, right?

She picked up the phone and thought about calling someone, just to get her mind off him. She knew Heather and Julie would both be working. She really didn't want to call John; he'd ask too many questions. Finally, she decided to call one of her old neighbors, Jill, who picked up after just a couple of rings.

"Hello?"

"Jill? This is Charlotte."

"Oh, my goodness! It's so good to hear from you! Dan and I were just talking about you last night, wondering how you're doing."

"Well, I'm doing pretty well, actually. In fact, I'm seriously considering moving back over there."

"Really? We wondered why the "for sale" sign had been removed. We were afraid you'd just given up on trying to sell it. So, you don't like The Falls?"

"Oh, I guess it's okay but it just isn't home, you know?"

"I imagine that's true. So, you sound great, Charlotte. When will we get to see you?"

"I'm not sure. I may be out of town for a few days, but probably shortly after that. I'll be sure to stop by and see you and Dan when I come over."

"What are you doing tonight?"

"Tonight?"

Jill laughed. "Yes. The Johnsons are having a little party over at their place tonight. It's their anniversary. All the neighbors have been invited. We could even pick you up, if you need a ride."

"Well…"

"Oh, come on, Charlotte, it would be fun. Everyone would love to see you."

"I don't have a gift for them, though."

"No problem. They said no gifts. Dan and I decided we'd take a bottle of wine, though, and we still need to pick one up. We could come get you, and stop and buy the wine on the way back. You could pick out a bottle of wine for them, too. You know how much fun we've always had at our little neighborhood parties. Please come!"

"You know what? You're right. I will come. What time?"

140

"I think they're starting around sevenish. We'll come get you about quarter 'til, will that work?"

"Absolutely. Thanks."

Charlotte provided directions to her apartment and asked Jill to text her when they arrived. She sure didn't want to be hanging around the lobby or outside the building, waiting for them. She'd feel safer waiting in her apartment until they arrived.

After the call, Charlotte got up and walked back to the French doors again. She peeked outside but didn't seem him anywhere. She hoped that meant he had left. Her phone rang again and she looked at the number; it was Jill again.

"Hello?"

"Charlotte? Listen, Dan and I were talking. Why don't you plan on staying in our guest room tonight? You know we'll all be drinking and these parties can sometimes go pretty late. We'll take you home any time you're ready tomorrow."

"That sounds perfect. If you're sure you don't mind, I'd love to do that.

"Great! We'll see you soon."

"Bye."

Well. That had turned out nicely. She'd get out of here and be with a group of friends. She'd feel safer. She just hoped he didn't follow them but knew that even if he did, he'd never show his face in front of all those people. He might feel tough enough to pick on a defenseless old woman, but he was too cowardly to try anything around other people. She went to her bedroom and packed an overnight bag, then changed clothes for the party.

This would be fun, seeing people from the old neighborhood. She still had a couple of hours to kill. Every ten minutes or so, she found herself looking out the peephole of the front door, or peeking out the blinds at the back. This was crazy. A glass of wine would sure help, but she remembered her promise to Lexi. She grabbed the bottle of wine out of the cabinet, opened it, and dumped the contents down the kitchen sink. She didn't want to be tempted. She decided that when she went to buy the wine for the party tonight, she'd buy herself some lemonade or something. If anyone offered her a drink, she'd just say she wasn't drinking alcohol due to her medications. She made herself a cup of tea, then settled back in the living room.

She decided to read for a while, but gave up after about fifteen minutes; it was just impossible to stay focused. She flipped on the TV and watched a couple of episodes of 'Seinfeld.' Then she switched over to the home decorating network Jade enjoyed so much. Before long, she found herself so engrossed in the program, that she lost track of time until her phone alerted her that she had a text message.

Hi. It's Dan. We're here. Would you like me to come up and walk you to the car?

That was a good idea. If he was lurking around watching, he wouldn't bother her with Dan nearby.

Yes, please. If you don't mind. I'm in 204.

K. Be right there.

A few minutes later, she and Dan were walking across the lobby toward the exit doors. She could see Jill in their car, right outside the front doors. She smiled and waved and Charlotte smiled back at her. She looked around as she and Dan walked toward the doors, but didn't see him anywhere. When they arrived at the car, Dan opened the passenger door for her.

"Oh, no, I can sit in back."

"Charlotte, come on, I insist. I'll sit in back."

As he closed the door, she turned to Jill to tell her hello. Not five feet away from the driver's side of the car, there he stood, hands in his pockets and a sick smile on his face. He nodded at her, turned, and walked back toward the parking lot. She felt shaken and Jill looked at her questioningly and asked, "Charlotte? What is it?" She turned and looked over her left shoulder then back at Charlotte. "Is something wrong?"

"Oh. No. No, I'm fine, I'm sorry. I just thought I saw someone I knew but it wasn't him. So, how are you, dear?"

"Doing great, Charlotte. Looking forward to this party, I can tell you. What a week I've had!"

As she pulled out of the driveway, Jill started telling Charlotte all about the challenges she'd faced at work this week. She had a way of making everything seem humorous and before long, the three of them were laughing and Charlotte had forgotten all about Douglas. Yes, this visit was exactly what she needed.

Chapter 28

The next few days were a flurry of activity. Charlotte had a wonderful time Friday evening at the Johnsons' anniversary party and was glad she'd agreed to stay with Jill and Dan. She felt secure in her old neighborhood, around old friends. She and Jill even went over to Charlotte's condo to look around and it felt so good to be there. She knew then she really did want to move back there. The next day, she had breakfast with Dan and Jill, then he drove her home. She called her kids, did some laundry, and started making more plans for the trip to Santa Fe. She had thought about renting a car, thinking it might be more difficult for Douglas to spot them, but then decided against it. Lexi would be doing all the driving, and as an inexperienced driver, Charlotte felt she'd more comfortable driving a car she was familiar with, rather than a rental.

She and the girls went to the jail on Saturday afternoon, and after the girls visited with their mother, Charlotte met with her alone. As Charlotte visited with Regina, she thought to herself, this woman is one tough cookie. It was obvious Regina wasn't sure if she could trust her, and Charlotte didn't blame her. Regina may have had her shortcomings, but she was their mother and it was natural of her to be suspicious. After some conversation, though, she agreed the girls could go to New Mexico with Charlotte. She also agreed to sign a power of attorney, allowing Charlotte to take Jade to Santa Fe, and giving her authority to seek medical care for her, if necessary. Such a document wouldn't be required for Lexi, since she was eighteen. Regina said they'd discuss guardianship after Charlotte and the girls returned from New Mexico. Charlotte agreed that was more than fair.

Regina's revocation hearing had been set but was still ten days away, so she figured she'd still be here at the county jail when they returned from their trip to Santa Fe. Charlotte thanked her, told her she'd return Monday morning with the paperwork, and left. Charlotte's attorney friend with the family courts had agreed to come back with her on Monday, to arrange for the paperwork to be signed and notarized. Lexi drove them back to Charlotte's apartment and the three of them had dinner in the dining hall. Lexi and Charlotte told Jade about the plan to go to Santa Fe and she was very excited. They didn't mention anything yet about the issue of guardianship, or what would happen if Regina went to prison, and Jade didn't bring it up, either. Charlotte figured there was plenty of time for that discussion, later.

On Sunday, Charlotte made hotel reservations in Santa Fe and called Debra to tell her they'd be there by Tuesday and would probably come by her place on Wednesday. She packed for the trip and cancelled her newspaper subscription. Monday morning, she spoke with Peter and told him she'd be away for a few days and asked that he continue to keep an eye out for Douglas. She asked him to call her, if there were any problems. Lexi and Jade showed up a little before nine, both with full backpacks. A little later, they were pulling out of the complex. Charlotte hadn't seen a trace of Douglas, nor heard from him since Friday. Maybe he'd given up and had gone home to Philadelphia. Hopefully, he hadn't decided to go back to Santa Fe, to visit Debra again.

Lexi drove back to the county jail, and Charlotte called her attorney friend.

"Hi, Carolyn, we're here."

"Okay. Are you parked?"

"Yes."

She explained where they were parked, and Carolyn provided directions to where she was waiting outside the building. They eventually found each other and went inside. The girls had elected to wait for her in the car. It was a good thing Carolyn had agreed to help. Charlotte couldn't imagine how she would have managed to have the Power of Attorney signed by a jail inmate, witnessed, and notarized without her assistance. It took a while, but about an hour later, she was back at the car.

"Girls, I'm so sorry that took so long. You had a long wait."

"It's okay, Ms. T. It was worth the wait if it means we get to go to New Mexico," replied Jade.

Charlotte smiled and held up the paperwork. "All set!"

The girls cheered and they were on their way. As Lexi drove, Charlotte told her they needed to make one more stop before heading out of Houston. She gave her directions and soon, they were entering the parking lot in front of the DMV.

Lexi parked, then turned to her and asked, "Charlotte? Why are we here?"

"So you can take your driving test."

"Now?!"

"No time like the present, as they say."

"Oh, my gosh. What if I fail?"

She shrugged. "Then you'll take it again, later. You'll still have your permit."

Lexi chewed on her lower lip and thought about it a moment.

"Okay. Let's do this," she said, and the three of them got out of the car and went inside.

Unfortunately, as is typical, they had a long wait before Lexi was finally called for her turn to take the test. It was impressive how patient Jade was at waiting; better than me, thought Charlotte. She just sat and read a book she'd brought with her and seemed oblivious to her surroundings. When Lexi left with the woman who would go with her on the driving test, she was obviously nervous. Charlotte was worried for her. Jade looked over at Charlotte, patted her hand, and said, "It'll be okay, Ms. T. She'll pass. She's a good driver, right?"

She smiled back at Jade. "You're right. Nothing to worry about."

Turns out, Jade was right. Lexi walked back up to them with a big grin on her face, waving a sheet of paper in front of them.

"I did it! I got my license!"

Jade jumped up and hugged her. "Phew! I was worried." She exclaimed. "I just knew you'd do something dumb, like hit another car or something."

"Why, you little faker!" Charlotte exclaimed.

Jade laughed. "Can we go to Santa Fe now, Ms. T?" she asked.

Charlotte nodded. "Let's go. I'm starving, though. When we get out of the city, let's keep an eye out for a Dairy Queen, okay?"

And that's what they did. By the time they finally managed to escape all the traffic in Houston and found a DQ on the outskirts of the city, it was close to two o'clock. They were famished and wolfed down burgers, fries, and ice cream sundaes. As they returned to the car, Lexi commented, "Well, we haven't gotten very far. We won't be to New Mexico by tonight, will we?"

"No, but that's okay. We'll stop along the way tonight, which I'd figured we'd do, anyway. Then we'll have all day tomorrow. It's not a problem," Charlotte replied.

With Jade's assistance from the back seat, Charlotte found a radio station and enjoyed listening to her sing along to most of the songs. Lexi seemed a bit nervous behind the wheel, at first, but soon seemed to relax and did very well with the driving. Jade seemed amazed by everything she saw, telling Charlotte she'd never been on a road trip before.

"Really? What's the furthest you've ever been from Houston?"

She shrugged. "Galveston, I guess."

"Oh? You've been to the beach, then?"

She nodded. "Lexi's grandma took us there once, didn't she, Lexi?"

"Yes. You were pretty little. You remember that?"

"Sure. I was scared of the waves, but you held on to me. And we found some seashells, remember?"

Lexi smiled. "I do. I wonder what ever happened to those seashells?"

"I don't know."

"Well, maybe one day I can take you girls to Florida, where my son lives, and you can see the beautiful beaches there. Or maybe even to California, where Heather is. The beaches are nice there, too."

"Really?! Wow! That would be awesome! And we could get more seashells!" exclaimed Jade.

"That's right." Charlotte replied.

"And maybe Regina can come, too," said Jade.

"Maybe." Charlotte glanced over at Lexi but saw no reaction. She just stared straight ahead, seemingly concentrating on her driving.

Chapter 29

A few hours later, they pulled into a gas station in Decatur, Texas. Charlotte handed a credit card to Lexi, who got out of the car. Jade also got out of the car and while Lexi filled the gas tank, Jade cleaned off the windshield. When they got back in the car, Charlotte smiled at them. "This is just like a full-service station. Next thing I know, you'll be checking the oil and tires."

"Huh? What's a full-service station?" asked Jade.

"Yeah, you wouldn't know anything about that. Never mind, it's not important. Girls, how about we stay in Decatur tonight? We can find a motel, have some dinner, and make an early night of it. That way, we can get an early start and be in Santa Fe by mid-afternoon."

They both agreed to her suggestion and soon found themselves checked in to a motel and eating at a restaurant next door. She tried not to let on, but was exhausted. She couldn't wait to get back to the motel and into bed. She looked at her watch; it was only seven-fifteen. She stifled a yawn and smiled up at the waitress as she approached their table.

"Anything else, ladies?" she asked.

Charlotte looked at the girls, who both shook their heads. "We're fine, thanks. I guess we're ready for our check."

"Yes, ma'am."

Soon, they were back in their room. Charlotte made sure the door was locked and the safety latch secured. The girls decided to have their showers tonight, while she just crawled into bed and told them she'd see them in the morning. She fell asleep to the sound of Lexi's shower and Jade's TV program, set at a low volume. A couple of times, she awoke to the sound of their voices, but fell right back to sleep.

Then, in the darkness, her eyes opened suddenly and she felt a chill. She wasn't sure if she'd heard something or if she'd been dreaming. The room was pitch black and she looked over to the other bed and saw that the girls were both sound asleep. Her heart was racing.

Why? Then, she heard it; the sound of the door knob being jiggled and a scratching noise on the door.

She reached over for her phone but before she could place a call to 911, she heard loud voices in the hall, and the sound of running footsteps. Then she heard what she thought were gunshots. Oh, my god, what was happening? Lexi sat up as Charlotte ran toward the front door and looked out the peephole.

"What was that?" asked Lexi.

"I'm not sure."

She went to her suitcase and found her robe. She grabbed the card key and told Lexi to wait in the room. By now, there were loud voices coming from the hall. As she opened the door a crack and peeked out, she saw a security guard and another employee at the end of the hall, looking down at a man lying on the ground. A few other motel guests were standing around in the hall, also looking over at the three men. Charlotte approached a couple standing nearby.

"What happened?"

"I'm not sure. I think that guy on the ground tried to break into a room and was shot."

"What?!"

As she made her way down the hall, sirens could be heard from outside, getting louder as emergency vehicles apparently got closer. She saw the security guard placing handcuffs on the man lying on the floor. Then he stood up, turned toward Charlotte and the other hotel guests standing in the hall, and asked that they return to their rooms.

"Show's over, folks. For your own safety, I ask that you clear the hall. The police are on their way, and may have questions. If any of you saw or heard anything, please go to the front desk and wait, as I'm sure the police will want to speak with you."

As he was speaking, Charlotte tried to get a look at the man lying on the floor. She wondered if he was still alive. Then, she saw his face and immediately recognized him. It was Dennis! He'd been trying to enter their room – that's what she'd heard at the door. She turned

150

and walked toward the front lobby. As she walked outside, police and EMT personnel were entering. One of the officers turned toward her.

"Ma'am? Where are you going?"

"Oh. I just want to get something from my car. I'll be right back."

She knew she probably looked foolish in her pajamas and robe, heading out to the parking lot, but the officer apparently didn't see her as threatening and waved her on. She walked out into the parking lot and looked around. There it was. The black pickup truck. She was sure it was his; it had the same toolbox and skull and cross bone stickers on the back window. She went back inside and headed to her room. When she got there, both girls were sitting on the bed and they both jumped up and rushed over to her as she entered the room, asking what had happened.

"I'm not sure. I think the security guard caught a burglar. But it's okay now. The police are here and the man's been arrested."

Lexi looked at her and raised an eyebrow but didn't ask any questions.

"Wow, this sure is starting out to be an exciting trip, Ms. T!" said Jade.

"You're right, Jade, it is."

Just then, there was a knock at their door. Charlotte looked out the peephole. It was a police officer and another man who appeared to be a motel employee. She opened the door.

"Yes?"

"Charlotte Tilian?"

"Yes."

The police officer held up his credentials and introduced himself as a deputy with the Wise County Sheriff's Office.

"May I ask you a few questions, please?"

"Certainly. But can we speak somewhere else? I'd like for the children to get back to bed."

"Of course. We can speak with you in the manager's office."

"Alright."

She turned back to the girls and told them she'd be right back, to try to get some sleep. She knew that wouldn't happen but didn't want to be questioned by the officer in front of them. As they got settled in the manager's office, the officer told her the security guard had thought the man who was arrested had been trying to break into Charlotte's room. He wanted to know if she'd heard anything.

"You know, I'm not sure. I woke up and wasn't sure if I'd heard something or if I'd been dreaming. Then I heard all of the commotion out in the hall."

"Commotion?"

"It sounded like people running, some shouts, what appeared to be gunshots."

"Do you recall what they were saying – the shouts, I mean?"

She thought about it. "Not exactly. Something like 'stop' or 'halt,' something along those lines, I think."

"Do you have any idea why someone would be breaking into your room?"

"Me, specifically?"

"That's right."

"No. Not really. I mean, I guess people break into motel rooms to steal items, so maybe if he was trying to break into our room, he was hoping we'd have something of value, I don't know. Or maybe he had more violent intentions."

"Yes, ma'am. Maybe."

He pulled out a notepad and read the name on it. "Dennis Kirkpatrick. That name mean anything to you?"

She frowned and shook her head. "No. Should it?"

"That's the suspect's name. Or at least, that's the name on his I.D. which also gives a Houston address. The manager here tells me you're from Houston."

She nodded. "That's right."

"Where are you headed, ma'am?"

"To Santa Fe."

"Vacation?"

"Yes. We're visiting the daughter of a friend of mine, who recently passed away."

"And the girls are your grandkids, I assume?"

"Not exactly."

"Oh?"

"Well, they're good friends. Their mother and I thought this would be a nice opportunity for them to see a little bit of the country. And Lexi is helping with the driving."

"So, you don't know anyone by the name of Dennis Kirkpatrick?"

"No, I don't."

"Sure seems coincidental, doesn't it?"

"Coincidental?"

"A guy tries to break into your room. You're both from Houston. Maybe the girls know him?"

"I wouldn't know, Officer. But I doubt it. Houston's an awfully big city, it really doesn't seem that odd to me that we both live in Houston; a lot of people live in Houston. Do you know anything about him?"

"Not really. Not yet."

"Is he going to be okay? I mean, was he shot? I did hear gunshots."

"He was shot. But it doesn't appear to be life-threatening. Why?"

"Oh, I don't have any kind of personal interest in him, Officer. It's just a bit unnerving, as you can imagine. Traveling with two young girls. A stranger tries to break into our room and ends up shot. I'm sure the girls will have questions about it."

He nodded. "I'd like to speak with the girls, too. Just to make sure they don't know the suspect."

"Is that really necessary? I mean, it's late, I'm hoping the girls can get some sleep before we leave. This Kirkpatrick character isn't going anywhere. Can't you speak with them later?"

He shook his head. "Afraid not."

She sighed. "Alright. I'll go get them."

"I'll walk back with you."

Crap. She had hoped to have a minute alone with them. They went back to the room and she opened the door. Lexi was sitting in a guest chair and Jade appeared to be sleeping in their bed. Lexi stood and started to walk toward Charlotte but stopped when she saw the officer. Charlotte motioned to her to step outside and Lexi followed them into the hallway, closing the door behind her.

"What's up, Charlotte?"

"This officer would like to ask you some questions. I told him I don't know the suspect, but he wants to make sure you and Jade don't know him."

"Ma'am?" he interrupted her. "I'd appreciate it if you'd let me do the talking, okay?"

"Oh. Yes, of course. I'm sorry."

He turned back toward Lexi, took down her name and date of birth and asked for the same information about her sister. He asked why she was traveling with Charlotte and seemed satisfied with her answer. Then he asked if she knew anyone by the name of Dennis Kirkpatrick.

Charlotte held her breath but Lexi maintained a poker face. She seemed to consider the name a moment, then shook her head and said it didn't sound familiar. He read the address that was on Dennis' driver's license.

"That address mean anything to you?"

"No, Sir. Just that it's weird that he's from Houston. I mean, we live in Houston, too."

"Yes, that is a little weird, huh? You sure you don't know this guy?"

He handed the license to Lexi and asked her to take a look at it. She shook her head.

"Nope. Don't know him." She handed it back to the officer. "Is he dead?"

154

"No, he'll live. But he'll be locked up for a while. He's already got a record, so hopefully, the judge will throw the book at him."

He handed Charlotte a business card and asked that she call him if she thought of anything else that might help the investigation. He also asked for her contact information, which she provided.

"I guess you can let your sister sleep. It's doubtful she'd know anything about this character, if you don't. But if it turns out she knows him, y'all call me, alright?"

"Oh, of course, Officer." Charlotte said. "Thank you. I'm so glad he didn't manage to break into our room. It's frightening to think of what could have happened."

"Well, I guess you need to thank the security guard here, he's the one who stopped the guy."

"Yes, I certainly will."

"Well, goodnight."

"Goodnight, Officer."

He walked off and Lexi turned to her.

"So, what if Dennis tells them the truth? They'll know we were lying about not knowing him."

"You're right. But do you really think he wants to admit to intent to harm two young girls and an old woman? He'd be better off saying he was just trying to burglarize the room, right?"

"Yeah. I'm just not sure if he's smart enough to figure that out, Charlotte."

"Well, hopefully his lawyer will be."

As they walked back into the room, Jade sat up in her bed.

"Is he gone?" she asked.

"Yes," answered Lexi. "You did good, Jade."

I looked at Lexi and she explained, "I told her to pretend she was asleep if any cops came by. She was kind of shook up."

"Oh. Well, Jade, you don't need to worry. Everything's okay now."

"Yes, ma'am. But I don't think I can go back to sleep now."

"Well, look, it's five o'clock. I think I'll have a quick shower. You girls get dressed and we'll go ahead and hit the road. Do you mind grabbing breakfast to go at McDonald's instead of waiting for the free breakfast here? They don't put the food out until six-thirty."

They both agreed and before long, they were on the road. They had a quick breakfast from a drive-through window and soon, were back on the highway and Charlotte was sipping her coffee. She looked at the clock on the dash – 5:40. A much earlier start than she'd hoped for.

Jade tapped her on the shoulder. "Ms. T?"

She turned to look back at her. "Yes, Jade?"

"Did you find out what happened back at the motel? Was a man really trying to break into a room?"

"Yes, it appears he was."

"Well, will we be safe in the hotel in Santa Fe? Do people try to break into rooms a lot?"

"Oh, I'm sure we'll be perfectly safe, don't worry. I don't think it happens very often, and besides, most hotels have security systems and officers on duty to keep everyone safe. That's what happened last night, Jade. The security guard probably saw the guy on a camera, then caught him breaking into a room, and stopped him."

"Oh. I wonder whose room he tried to break into. I'll bet they were scared."

Charlotte nodded. "Yes. I'm sure they were. Very scared."

Chapter 30

As they approached New Mexico, Jade got excited. "Look, we're only five miles from New Mexico, Ms. T! When we get to the border, can we stop and take pictures? I wonder what it will look like!"

Charlotte smiled. "Yes, we can do that. It won't look much different than it does now, but there should be a sign welcoming us to the Land of Enchantment. I'll take your picture in front of that sign, okay?"

"The Land of Enchantment! It sounds wonderful, doesn't it? Have you been there before?"

"Yes, I have. It will take us a while to reach some scenic areas, but you'll be able to see some beautiful country while we're in New Mexico. I hope you enjoy Santa Fe as much as I always do."

When they reached the border, they stopped and she took a photo of the two girls in front of the sign welcoming them to New Mexico. They took advantage of the nearby rest stop then got back on the road. Jade asked some questions about Santa Fe and they had a long conversation about some of the places Charlotte had been to and what they might do during their trip.

Along the way, they stopped a few times for breaks. They'd get a drink and walk around a bit to stretch their legs. Charlotte was impressed by how well Lexi was doing at driving this long trip and thanked her several times. She'd just shake her head and tell her she was the one who should be thanking her. By three-thirty, they were driving into Santa Fe. The navigation system helped them locate the lodge quite easily. The adobe lodge sat high on a hill on the outskirts of town and was just beautiful with desert landscaping and brightly covered flowers near the entry way.

Lexi parked and Jade unbuckled her seatbelt. "Wow, Ms. T! This place looks awesome! Are we really staying here?!"

She laughed. "Yes, Jade, we're really staying here."

They gathered their belongings and made their way inside the lodge. As they were walking in, a young couple walked toward them with a little chihuahua on a leash. The dog had on a pink collar with sparkling rhinestones.

"Oh, look! Isn't she cute?!" exclaimed Jade. She looked up at the woman holding the leash. "Can I pet your dog, please?"

"Well, let me hold her. She's kind of nervous and I'm never sure how she'll react to strangers. But if I hold her and you just place your hand in front of her out flat to let her sniff at it first, she should be fine."

Jade followed her instructions and soon was petting the little dog and laughing when it licked her fingers. "What's her name?"

"Her name is Cassi."

"Oh, that's a pretty name. I hope I see you again, little Cassi."

Jade said goodbye to the dog and the three of them walked up to the front desk. Soon, they were walking into their suite.

Jade and Lexi were both very impressed by the rooms and by the view over the courtyard below.

"Wow, this is the nicest place I've ever seen, Ms. T," said Jade as she looked out the window. She turned back to the room and held her hands out wide. "And look how big this place is! It's bigger than our apartment, isn't it, Lexi?"

"Yeah. And a helluva lot nicer."

"Lexi! Don't cuss," admonished Jade.

"Sorry. But it is. A *heck* of a lot nicer. Better?"

Jade smiled. "Yes!" She looked back outside. "Ms. T, will we be able to swim while we're here?"

"Sure. Why not?"

"Really?! Like now?"

"Hey, goof ball," said Lexi. "You gonna go skinny dipping? I think they probably frown on that here."

Jade looked disappointed. "Oh, yeah. That's right. We don't have swimsuits."

"Well, we need to rectify that." Charlotte said.

"What's rectify?" asked Jade.

"Correct it. Go get swimsuits."

"Oh. That would be really cool." She looked up at Lexi. "Do we have enough money, Lexi?"

Charlotte interrupted Lexi before she could even answer.

"Don't worry about it. Come on, let's go. We'll ask at the front desk where we might shop for swim suits. My treat."

It was fun shopping with Lexi and Jade. The hardest part was getting them to stop looking at the price tags and putting back anything they thought was too expensive. Finally, they each found a couple they liked and Charlotte continued looking around the store while they went to the dressing rooms to try on the suits. She selected some beach towels and flip flops for all three of them and after they left the department store, they shopped at a drug store for sun block, magazines, and cheap sunglasses for the girls.

Soon, Charlotte was lounging by the pool with a tall lemonade and a magazine. The girls were enjoying the pool, which was practically empty. After a while, some other people showed up and soon Jade had made friends with another little girl. Lexi got out of the pool and dried off, then lay back on the lounger next to Charlotte's. She put on her sunglasses and lay back.

"This is nice, Charlotte. Really relaxing."

"Yes, it is."

"So, I was thinking…"

"Yes?"

"You think we could get somebody to shoot Douglas now?"

Charlotte turned to her with a shocked look on her face. Lexi just laughed.

"I'm kidding, Charlotte. Geez!"

Charlotte shook her head and smiled. "Well. I must admit. It wouldn't hurt my feelings any if something happened to him, too."

Lexi nodded. "Yeah. One down, one to go."

Charlotte looked over at her and Lexi just smiled. "One can dream, right, Charlotte?"

Chapter 31

That evening, they went to the plaza and walked around for a bit before enjoying a wonderful dinner of traditional Santa Fe style Mexican food. She *so* wanted a margarita with her meal, but settled for iced tea. As they ate, they discussed their plans for the next day.

"I'll call Debra after dinner and ask when she'd like to meet with me. Afterward, we can do some sightseeing. Any ideas on what you'd like to do?" She knew they'd been looking through travel brochures at the lodge earlier today.

Jade nodded. "I'd like to see Ghost Ranch. And go to the Georgia O'Keefe museum. Would that be too much?"

"No, that wouldn't be too much. Those are good choices. Lexi?"

"Well, I like Jade's choices. And maybe we could drive up to the ski area. I know there isn't any snow this time of year, but the pictures still looked pretty."

"It is pretty. If we have time this week, is there anywhere else you'd like to go? Taos, maybe?"

"We could go that far?"

"It's not really that far. We might be able to go there."

"Great. Thanks."

"You're welcome."

Later that evening, she called Debra, who invited the three of them to breakfast the next day. They made plans to meet at her home at nine o'clock. Charlotte asked if she'd heard from her father.

"Yes. He called me last night and said he's back in Philadelphia. I didn't ask him about you, Charlotte. Did he ever meet up with you in Houston?"

"No. He didn't."

"Oh. Well, I wonder what he was doing there, then. It's all very strange."

"Yes, it is."

They said goodbye and she considered what Debra had said. So, was Douglas really in Philadelphia? In this age of cell phone use, it was impossible to know. He could have called her from anywhere.

Chapter 32

The next morning found them on their way to Debra's home. Charlotte had programmed the address in the navigation system, and Lexi was driving. Jade was in the back seat, humming along to the local radio station and looking out the window.

"I love all the adobe houses, don't you, Ms. T?"

"They're nice, aren't they?"

"Why don't we have adobe houses in Houston?"

"Well, I haven't ever really thought about it, Jade, but I'm guessing it has something to do with our climate and local resources."

"We probably have too much rain, right?"

"Maybe so. Maybe we can learn more about adobe while we're here."

Pretty soon, they were pulling into the driveway in front of Debra's home. "Yay, she has an adobe house!" exclaimed Jade.

Charlotte rang the doorbell and they waited on the front step for Debra to answer. When she opened the door, Charlotte was taken aback at how much she resembled Carla. She smiled at her.

"I'd know you anywhere, Debra."

Debra laughed and said, "I know, I know. I get that all the time. I don't think we really look that much alike, but other people seem to think so. I'll take it as a compliment."

"As you should. Your mom was a beautiful woman – and so are you!"

"Thanks. Well, come in."

She closed the door and turned toward Lexi. "You must be Lexi. I'm Debra Briones. Pleased to meet you." She held out her hand for Lexi and they shook hands. Then she tuned to Jade. "And look at you – cute as a button! Are you Jade?"

"Yes, ma'am." She shook Debra's hand and looked around. "I like your adobe house."

"Thank you. I wasn't too sure about having an adobe house, at first, but it's practically impossible to find anything else around here. Now that we've lived in it a few months, I love it. I especially like all the tile and wood – hardly anyone has carpet here."

"Your home is lovely, Debra," Charlotte told her.

They walked into the kitchen and a very handsome man stood up from the table and walked toward them.

"Well, hello ladies!"

Debra introduced them to her husband, Julio and explained he had taken the morning off so he could meet them. Debra invited them to sit at the table, saying she hoped they liked Mexican food. Breakfast consisted of flour tacos with their choice of chorizo, egg, cheese and a variety of salsas, as well as a nice selection of fresh fruit and orange juice. There was also a carafe of coffee on the table. The meal was delicious and they enjoyed the conversation as Debra and Julio told them about moving from California to New Mexico. Debra said they had two daughters – sixteen-year-old twins – who were visiting Julio's parents in Sacramento. They would be home tomorrow and she hoped her daughters would have an opportunity to meet them before they returned to Houston.

"Maybe we could all meet for dinner one evening. What all do you plan to do while you're here? she asked.

"Well, the girls and I have decided we'd like to go out to Ghost Ranch, visit the O'Keefe museum, and drive up to the ski area. We may also drive over to Taos, if we have time."

"Oh, Taos is great. Have you been there?"

"I have but I'd like to take Jade and Lexi."

Julio nodded. "It's a lot different from Houston, that's for sure."

Jade turned to him. "I like it here. Mr. Briones, do you like it, too? Or do you miss California?"

"Oh, I like it. But I also miss California. My parents live there, so mostly, I miss them."

"That's like Miss Charlotte. She's far away from her family, too," replied Jade.

Soon, they were finished with breakfast and the girls started clearing off the table. Julio helped them, and Debra asked Charlotte to join her in their study. When they got to the study, she sat at the desk and offered Charlotte a seat on a futon across from the desk.

"So. I want to show you the paperwork concerning the funds Mom left for you."

"Alright."

She handed Charlotte a large envelope containing a stack of papers. Charlotte pulled them from the envelope and started reading through them then saw the figures and looked over at Debra in shock.

"This can't be real!"

"Oh, it's real."

"But this is — so..."

"Much?"

She nodded.

"I know. It's pretty incredible."

She shuffled through the papers. "Oh, my. Your father must be livid."

Debra laughed. "I'd guess that's an understatement."

"But why would she leave me such a fortune, Debra? It doesn't make sense."

"Look at page eleven, Charlotte."

She turned to page eleven and started to read. She nodded. Now it made sense.

"Alright, then. What do I do next?"

Debra handed her a business card. "Her attorney in Philadelphia suggests you visit this law firm in Santa Fe while you're here. They're also handling my inheritance for me. The two law firms have been in touch with each other, and this local firm can handle things for you, while you're in town. Or if you prefer to wait until you return to Texas, call the Philadelphia attorney and she'll connect you with someone in Houston."

"This is quite a responsibility, Debra."

"I know. But she knew you could handle the responsibility, that's why she chose you to do this. It's also pretty awesome, isn't it?" she smiled.

"Just like Carla."

Debra's eyes teared up and she nodded. "Yes. Just like Mom."

"Well, I have a lot to think about. And two girls waiting on me to show them around New Mexico. So, we'll get out of your hair but I'll call you again tomorrow, okay? As you said earlier, maybe we can get together for dinner one evening. I know the girls would enjoy meeting your daughters."

"That sounds great, Charlotte. Is there anything I can do for you while you're here?"

"I don't think so, but thanks."

They walked out of the study and back to the kitchen but Julio and the girls were gone. Debra pointed out the sliding glass doors off the living area. "There they are. I should've known."

They walked outside and found them standing around a huge telescope. Julio was explaining how it worked. As Debra slid the door closed, Julio turned and looked over at them.

"Hi. I was just telling the girls they need to come back at night to do some star-gazing. The night sky here is just spectacular."

"Can we, Charlotte?" Lexi asked.

She hadn't seen her this excited about anything. "Well, I'm sure we can do that, yes. Thanks, Julio."

"Are you kidding? It will be a thrill to share this with someone who's actually interested. Lexi here is quite the scientist, isn't she?"

Lexi blushed and Jade spoke up. "She's really smart, too, Mr. Briones. She's gonna go to college."

"Well, that doesn't surprise me. What do you plan to study, Lexi?" asked Julio.

"I'm not sure yet. Something to do with science."

"Any idea which field?"

"Well, I'd like to eventually work on something to do with the environment, like climate change, alternative energy sources, maybe oceanography. I really need to research my options some more."

"That sounds great. We need bright young women such as yourself to save our planet. Good for you, Lexi." Julio answered.

Lexi blushed again and Jade spoke up. "Thanks for showing us your telescope, Mr. Briones. I had no idea we could actually see planets until you showed us. It's really cool."

"You're welcome, Jade."

"Well, we should probably be on our way," Charlotte told Debra and Julio. "We have a lot to do while we're here. Thank you both so much for your hospitality and the wonderful breakfast."

"Oh, we were glad to have you here. We'll see you again soon, okay?" Debra hugged each of them and then walked them back inside and to the front door. They said their goodbyes and returned to the car.

As Lexi started the car, she looked over at her. "They were really nice, Charlotte."

"Yes, they were."

"How long did you know her mother?"

"Why, I don't remember ever not knowing her. We grew up together, lived in houses across the street from each other as little girls."

"But you never met Debra before today?"

Charlotte shook her head. "I'm afraid not. After Carla married, I only saw her every couple of years when we'd get together for trips to different places. I never visited her home."

"Did she visit yours?"

"Yes, a few times. But always by herself. Her family didn't accompany her."

"That seems strange."

"Well, she had a strange marriage."

"Sounds like it. So, where am I driving to now?"

She looked at the time. "How about the O'Keefe Museum?"

"Yay!" exclaimed Jade.

They thoroughly enjoyed the museum, especially Jade. While there, she also obtained more information about other places to see, including sights at Abiquiu and things to do at the Ghost Ranch. As they left the museum, Jade pointed out some information on a pamphlet she held.

"Look, Ms. T, we can go on a bus tour or a trail ride at the ranch. And there's a general store in Abiquiu where Georgia O'Keefe used to go, and we can get drinks and burgers there. That would be fun, right?"

"That does sound like fun, Jade. I think maybe we need an entire day to see the ranch and Abiquiu, don't you?"

"Yes, ma'am, I think you're right. So, what should we do this afternoon?"

"How about we have lunch and visit some of the shops and artists' booths in and around the plaza? Then Lexi could drive us up to the ski area. After that, maybe we should return to the lodge and you girls can swim again, if you like. Then we'll go to Abiquiu and the Ghost Ranch tomorrow. How does that sound?"

"That sounds awesome, Ms. T."

"Lexi, what do you think? Does this plan work for you, too?"

"Absolutely."

So, that's what they did. While the girls were strolling through the plaza, looking in shops, she took a break on a bench under a tree, pulled out the business card Debra had given her, and made a call to the Santa Fe law office. She made an appointment for early Friday morning. She then called Debra back and asked if they could meet them for dinner tomorrow night. Debra suggested a restaurant and they agreed to meet there tomorrow night at eight o'clock. She told Charlotte she'd make a reservation.

The rest of the afternoon was lovely. They enjoyed their lunch and the girls really enjoyed seeing the Native American jewelry displayed in the plaza, and the works of local artists for sale. The drive to the ski area was nice and they enjoyed the cooler temperatures. She

168

was wishing she'd thought to bring jackets with them but they didn't stay long. Later, she relaxed again on a chaise while the girls swam in the pool at the lodge. She felt like she might be getting a bit of a sunburn so applied more sunblock and looked over at the girls. Their complexions were much darker than hers, but she knew that didn't mean they were immune to skin damage from the sun. She called them over and asked them to put on some sunblock.

As Lexi was rubbing lotion on Jade's shoulders, Jade looked over at her. "Ms. T, your nose is really red. I think you have a sunburn."

She sighed. "Yes, I think you're right. I didn't remember to put sun block on in time. I'm afraid I burn quite easily."

"Does it hurt?"

"No, not really."

"That's good."

Jade jumped back in the pool and Lexi lay back on her chaise. "This is the life, huh, Charlotte?"

She smiled. "Not too shabby."

Chapter 33

Thursday was a great day. She really enjoyed seeing everything again through the eyes of Jade and Lexi and realized she hadn't fully appreciated just how special the area was, until she shared it with them. They went on one of the landscape bus tours while at the Ghost Ranch, and saw many of the places famously painted by Georgia O'Keefe. Jade took lots of pictures, using a digital camera Charlotte had brought along, and said she was going to use them as inspiration to create some of her own paintings when she got home. They agreed to save the trail ride for another time, when Charlotte would feel strong enough to join them. Jade admitted she was a little afraid of horses, anyway, and didn't seem at all disappointed in not doing the trail ride during this trip.

They went to Abiquiu and as Jade had suggested, had lunch at the general store.

"Can you believe we're sitting in the same exact place as Georgia O'Keefe once sat, Ms. T? Isn't that crazy?" exclaimed Jade.

"Pretty crazy, alright. And one day, another little girl will say, 'Can you believe we're sitting in the same exact place as that artist, Jade Romero once sat?'"

Jade giggled. "Do you really think I could be a famous artist one day, Ms. T?"

"I don't think so, I know so. You're very talented, Jade. If you follow your passion and work hard, you can do anything you want."

"And maybe I'll live here. But I'll visit you and Lexi. And Regina. Or maybe she'd move here and live with me. We'd have a nice, big adobe house in the mountains and I'd paint all day and make lots of money and take care of my mom so she wouldn't have to worry about money or anything."

Charlotte glanced at Lexi, who rolled her eyes. If Jade noticed, she didn't let on and asked, "Would you visit me if I moved here, Ms. T?"

"Jade, I'd visit you so often, you'd get sick of me."

Jade laughed. "I'd never get sick of you, Ms. T. You're too nice. Isn't she nice, Lexi?"

"She sure is, Jade. Nicest person I've ever met, that's for sure," replied Lexi.

After their day of sightseeing, they returned to the lodge and got ready for dinner. Lexi drove them to the restaurant Debra had recommended and when they entered the front door, they found the Briones family waiting just inside. Julio told the hostess they had arrived and she led the group to their table. After everyone was seated, Debra introduced them to their daughters, Sophie and Shelli. The dinner and the company were wonderful but Charlotte was tiring after the long day and was relieved when they finally got up to leave around nine-thirty. As they walked toward the front door, she quietly mentioned to Debra that she had an appointment with the lawyer at eight-thirty the next day.

"That's great. Let me know if I can help in any way."

"I will. Thank you." She turned to Julio. "And thank you for the lovely dinner. I hadn't intended for you to pay for our meal, but I certainly appreciate it."

"You're very welcome. Would tonight be a good time for the girls to do some star-gazing at our house?"

Before she could answer, Lexi spoke up. "Thanks, Mr. Briones, but Charlotte has an early appointment tomorrow, then we're thinking of going to Taos. We should probably get back to our room, right, Charlotte?"

She couldn't tell if Lexi had given that reply for her benefit, or if Lexi truly wanted to go back to the room already. She didn't want her and Jade to miss out on anything due to her fatigue. She decided to agree with Lexi for now, then verify what she and Jade thought when they had some privacy.

"You're probably right, Lexi. But thank you, Julio, for the offer."

They said their goodbyes and once they were settled in the car, she asked Lexi and Jade if they had wanted to go back to the home of Debra and her family, or if they really wanted to go back to the room.

"If you're worried about me, don't. You can drop me off at the room, spend an hour or two over there, then come back to the lodge."

Lexi looked back at Jade. "I don't know. What do you think, Jade?"

"If we don't go tonight, can we go another night?"

"I don't know," answered Lexi.

"Well, I'd kind of like to go, then," answered Jade.

Lexi turned back to Charlotte. "Are you sure? You won't mind being alone at the lodge?"

"I'll be fine, Lexi."

"And you think it's – you know – a good idea for us to go over there? I mean, you know…the thing with Debra's dad and all…"

"What thing?" asked Jade.

"Never mind," replied Lexi.

"Tell me!"

"If you want to go over there, you'd better just be quiet," said Lexi, more sternly than Charlotte had ever heard her speak to her sister. Jade just crossed her arms and looked out the window.

"I don't care what we do," she mumbled.

"Lexi, I'll call Debra and ask her if it's too late to accept the invitation, alright?"

"If you're sure," she answered.

Charlotte called Debra, who said of course the girls could come over, and that Sophie and Shelli had been disappointed when they thought they weren't coming. So, Lexi took Charlotte back to the lodge but wouldn't just leave her at the front of the hotel. She insisted that she and Jade would walk her back to the suite. As they entered the rooms, Jade ran toward the restroom. Lexi walked around the suite, checking that everything looked okay.

"Lexi, I'm sure we're safe. Debra said her father is back in Philadelphia."

"I know, but we can't be sure about that, can we?"

Charlotte looked over at the room's phone, sitting on the night stand by her bed; a light on it was blinking, indicating a message. She checked the message and learned that they'd had a visitor this evening who had left a written note for her at the front desk. She told Lexi.

"You wait here, Charlotte. I'll go get the message. I'll be right back. I've got my card key, so don't answer the door if anyone knocks, okay?"

"Okay. Be careful."

A few minutes later, Lexi returned to the room with an envelope in her hand. By then, Jade was impatiently waiting, wanting to go over to Debra's. Lexi handed the envelope to Charlotte and she opened it. There was a short note: *Sorry I missed you. Maybe tomorrow? DW*

Charlotte sat down on the bed and held the note up for Lexi to read.

She read the note and looked at Charlotte. "Okay. Jade and I are staying here tonight."

Jade started to protest but Lexi stopped her. "Jade, I know you don't understand this, but just trust me. Charlotte needs for us to stay with her, okay?"

Jade nodded. "Okay."

Charlotte knew there was no point in arguing with Lexi, and if she was honest with herself, knew she was relieved they weren't going over to Debra's house. She called Debra and apologized, saying they'd had a long day and had decided it would be best to just get to bed as early as possible. Debra said she understood and they agreed they'd speak again after Charlotte's meeting with the attorney.

As tired as she was, she didn't get a lot of sleep that night. Every little sound woke her and she never did sleep soundly. At six o'clock, she gave up and had her shower and got dressed. Soon, she heard the girls getting up and going in their restroom to get ready. She made coffee in the room, sat on the couch that was in the living area adjoining her room with the girls' room, and looked through some travel magazines.

Jade peeked in and asked if she could come in. "Of course! Good morning! Why, you're up and dressed early!"

She smiled. "I know. I can't wait to go to Taos."

"Same here. Are you hungry?"

"Yes, ma'am, a little. But Lexi said you have an appointment downtown so we don't have time to go to the restaurant for breakfast."

"Well, there's a bookstore with a coffee shop near the office I'm going to this morning. We can stop in there before my appointment and I'll grab a pastry or something. You girls can stay and have breakfast and check out the bookstore while I'm at my appointment, if you like."

"Oh, that sounds nice!" said Jade. "Maybe I can find some books about adobe houses or Taos."

"I'll bet there's a good chance you might."

"What time do we need to go?" asked Jade.

She looked over at the bedside alarm clock. "In about thirty minutes. They open at eight."

"Okay. I'll go tell Lexi."

As she was finishing her coffee, Lexi and Jade both walked in and she told Lexi there was coffee, if she wanted some. Lexi started to pour herself some coffee and turned to Jade.

"Hey, Dude, they have packets of hot chocolate here. Want me to make a cup for you?"

"Yes, please."

After they finished their drinks, they gathered their belongings and left the room. The girls had their backpacks on their backs and Lexi pulled Charlotte's suitcase behind her. Soon, they were seated in the coffee shop and Charlotte was wolfing down a blueberry muffin while the girls sipped their drinks and waited on their food. As she took one last bite of the muffin, she wiped off her sticky hands the best she could then stood.

"Well, girls, I'm off to see the lawyer. I don't think it will take long. I'm going to leave you my phone, though, just in case you need anything. Here's the lawyer's name and number."

She showed Lexi the contact in her phone. "And here's Debra's name and number. If you have any problems, just call, okay?"

Lexi took the phone. "Thanks, Charlotte, but we'll be fine. Are you sure you don't need me to drive you? I don't feel right about you walking over there alone."

"I'm sure. It's just the next block over, and nobody will bother me in broad daylight with other people on the street. I also doubt you'd find any parking anywhere closer than this, anyway. You two have fun."

She put some money down on the table. "This should cover breakfast and a couple of books, if you find anything."

As Lexi started to protest, Charlotte just smiled and waved goodbye. She turned and walked out of the shop. After a short walk, during which she kept a constant lookout for Douglas, she entered the law office with five minutes to spare. The appointment went well and by nine-fifteen, she was on her way back to the bookstore/coffee shop. As she walked around the store, looking for the girls, she heard a familiar voice calling her name. She turned in the direction of the voice and saw Zelma, the bookstore's owner.

"Why, Charlotte Tilian! What a surprise! How are you?" She gave Charlotte a hug and pulled back and smiled down at her. Zelma was very tall; about six-two, Charlotte guessed.

"Oh, Zelma, it's wonderful to see you. How are you?"

"Great, great! Busy, as usual. What are you doing in Santa Fe? A workshop?"

"No, I'm here on a little vacation with two young friends. In fact, I'm looking for them now. I left them here while I had an appointment down the street, and I'm sure they're having a ball looking for books in your lovely store."

"How long will you be here?"

175

"Well, let's see. We're headed to Taos today. I'm not sure if we'll spend the night there or come back here tonight, it depends how much we are able to do today."

"What are you doing Sunday?"

"I'm not sure. In fact, we may leave Sunday."

"Oh, no! You have to stay!"

"Why's that, Zelma?"

"We're having an event here on Sunday afternoon. We're hosting some local authors and artists. I'd love if you could come, too. We'd put some of your books on display, of course. Would you mind coming and speaking briefly, maybe answering some questions from our customers?"

She considered Zelma's request. Zelma had always been a big supporter of her work and had carried her books before most other bookstores did. Then, she had an idea.

"Okay, Zelma, on one condition."

"Anything!"

"I'd like some publicity."

"Publicity?"

"Yes. You know — advertise that I'll be here. And that I'll have an exciting announcement to make."

Zelma grinned. "A new book?!"

"It's a surprise."

Zelma clapped her hands. "Oh, this is wonderful! Thank you! Here, let me give you all the details."

They walked up to one of the store's counters and Zelma reached for a flier about Sunday afternoon's event. They visited a while, then Charlotte located the girls in a reading corner. Jade jumped up when she saw her and ran over toward her.

"Look, Ms. T — this book has tons of pictures from Taos and information on things to see!"

"Well, that's great! Are you ready to head that way?"

"Now?!"

"Yes." She looked at her watch. "It's close to ten o'clock. We should get there right about lunch time."

Chapter 34

The drive to Taos took a while because they kept stopping to take in the beautiful scenery and take photos. She had brought the camera again and they already had a ton of photos. Of course, of the three of them, Jade managed to take the best photos; she just had a creative eye.

They had a late lunch when they arrived in Taos, and discussed what to do next. They went to the historic district and the plaza, looking through art galleries and shops. They found an ice cream shop and as they were enjoying their ice cream cones on a bench in the plaza, Jade asked if they were going back to Santa Fe that night.

"Well, it's already almost three o'clock and we haven't done much yet. Maybe we should see if we can get a room here so we can spend tomorrow here, too."

"That would be awesome, Ms. T, but what about our room back in Santa Fe? You already paid for that and it's just sitting empty. We don't want to waste your money."

She nodded. "That wasn't very good planning on my part, was it, Lexi? But it also seems like a waste of time and gas to come all the way to Taos and not do everything we'd like to do while we're here."

"Good point," said Jade.

She and Lexi laughed at Jade's serious expression, but when Charlotte was finished with her ice cream, she used her phone to look up local motels.

"Why don't I see if the Hotel La Fonda has any available rooms?"

"The one where D. H. Lawrence painted?" asked Jade excitedly.

"So, you've read about that, huh?"

"Yes, ma'am. That would be cool."

She checked but, unfortunately, they didn't have any vacancies. She had figured it was a long shot with such short notice. She ended up reserving a room at a motel about five miles from downtown.

"I'm sorry. The next time we come to Taos, I'll plan ahead and find somewhere really unique to stay."

"Well, we're staying in a super nice place in Santa Fe, Charlotte. And believe me, if you saw our apartment back home, you wouldn't be apologizing for anywhere we stay out here," replied Lexi.

"So, what do you want to do next?" Charlotte asked.

Lexi looked over at her sister. "Tour Guide Jade?" she asked.

Jade smiled. "There's the Taos Pueblo. People lived there over a thousand years ago and some people still live there now. Or the San Francisco de Assisi Mission Church. We could also drive out to see the Rio Grande Gorge Bridge. Oh, Lexi, there's something you'd really love – the Earthship Biotecture World Headquarters!"

"The what?!" Lexi and Charlotte both asked.

"Look. Here's a brochure."

Jade pulled out a little pamphlet that described the museum and visitors center, designed to showcase sustainability and environmental issues.

"Wow, that's pretty neat," said Lexi. "What time do they close?"

"Oh, I don't think we really have time today to go there. It closes at five."

"What time does it open tomorrow?" Charlotte asked.

"Ten."

"Well, why don't we go there in the morning? And if you girls think you'd enjoy it, we can reserve a spot for you to go river rafting tomorrow afternoon."

"Really?!" Jade was so excited. "We can really do that?!"

She smiled. "I think it would be a shame to come here and not enjoy the outdoors, don't you?"

"What about you, Charlotte? Are you up to a river raft trip?" asked Lexi.

"No, I don't think so. But that's okay. I'll just visit some art galleries or do some shopping. Don't worry about me."

They spent the remainder of the day at the San Francisco de Assisi Mission Church, then the Hacienda del Sol, once known as Los Gallos, where socialite and writer, Mabel Dodge Luhan had lived and entertained writers and artists of her time, predominantly in the 1920's. That evening after dinner when they were in their room, they started talking about the next day's plans. It had turned out that the raft trip would be in the morning, then they'd go to the Earthship Biotecture after lunch.

Early the next morning, they drove to the site where the girls would start their rafting trip. Charlotte paid and signed the necessary release form, then they got back in the car so Lexi could take her back to town. Lexi drove her to the plaza, then she and Jade went back to the river rafting site. Charlotte found a little coffee shop and settled down at a table with the local newspaper. It was still early and there weren't a lot of people on the plaza yet. It was nice, sitting and relaxing, enjoying a cup of good coffee. She realized that she was actually happy. Wow. It had been a long time since she'd felt that emotion – happiness.

She smiled and looked around. There were couples, young families, even a few other people sitting alone, as she was. She wondered about their lives. Were they happy? Certainly, they each had their own set of problems or challenges, heartbreaks and loving relationships. People could certainly be complicated.

After a while, she left the coffee shop and browsed through a couple of art galleries. She kept an eye out for Douglas, but never saw him. Hopefully, he hadn't followed them here. Soon, it was close to time for the girls' rafting trip to be finished. She made her way back to the coffee shop and sat outside. It wasn't long before she saw the girls walking toward her. Jade waved excitedly when she spotted her and she waved back. Jade ran up to her and gave her a hug.

"Oh, Ms. T, that was the best thing ever! Thank you, thank you, thank you!"

She laughed. "So, you had a good time?"

"It was awesome!"

Lexi walked up, smiling and Jade turned toward her.

"Wasn't it awesome, Lexi?"

"Pretty awesome," she replied.

"I was a little scared at first, but then it was just fun. The guide said we weren't on the roughest rapids and I'm glad, I think I'd be too scared to go there. Did you know they even have rafting trips that last three days? Can you imagine, Charlotte? Wouldn't that be cool, rafting on the river during the day and camping in a tent at night?"

"It would be."

"I've never camped in a tent, Ms. T. Have you?"

"Yes, I have. But it's been a long time."

"Did you like it?"

"Yes, I did. It was fun. Maybe you'll have a chance to go camping sometime."

Jade nodded. "Maybe. Did you have fun while we were on the raft, Ms. T"?

"Yes, I had a very nice time, thank you."

"What did you do?"

"Well, I sat in the coffee shop and read the paper for a while. I visited a couple of art galleries and looked in some shops. Then I came out here and sat on this bench and just did some people-watching for a while."

"What now?" asked Jade.

"I guess we should head back to the motel and check out, then go have lunch, and then go to the Earthship thing."

"Sounds good," said Lexi. "What time do we need to leave for Santa Fe?"

"Oh, I don't know. We don't need to be in any hurry. We just need to get back sometime tonight."

"Yes, ma'am."

The afternoon was very enjoyable. She was glad that Lexi was getting to do something that centered on her interests – science and the environment. Up until today, a good part of the trip had centered around the arts, which had really appealed more to her and Jade. That evening, as they headed back to Santa Fe, she found it difficult to keep her eyes open and kept nodding off. Finally, Lexi was gently nudging her arm and she woke to find they were in the parking lot of their lodge in Santa Fe.

"Oh, dear. I'm sorry, Lexi."

"It's okay, Charlotte. You were tired."

"Yes, I guess I was. It's a good thing you passed your driving test. I'm afraid I wouldn't be much use to you if you were still driving on a learner's permit!"

They got out of the car and gathered their belongings, then entered the lodge and rode the elevator to their suite. It felt good to be back. Jade ran over to the window and looked out.

"Ms. T, can we go swimming? There are people out there."

"Jade! Didn't you see that Charlotte is tired? We've already done a lot today."

"I'm sorry. You're right." Jade went off to their room, pulled her Taos book from her backpack, and lay on her bed to look at the book.

Charlotte looked over at Lexi. "If you want to go swimming, it would be okay with me if the two of you go for a while. It's up to you."

"Honestly, Charlotte, I think I'd rather pass. I'm kind of beat, too."

"Are you hungry?"

"A little. Are you?"

"Yes, but I don't feel like leaving this room now. How about ordering pizza?"

"That sounds good to me. Jade loves pizza, too."

So, they ordered pizza and watched some television. When she went to bed, the girls were still up, watching TV. The next morning, they all slept in later than usual. They decided to go for a swim, then to the lodge's Sunday brunch in their restaurant. The food was delicious.

As they were getting ready for the event at the bookstore, Charlotte's cell phone rang. She looked at the number; it was Debra.

"Hello, Debra. How are you?"

"I'm fine, thanks. Have you and the girls been having a good time?"

"We sure have." She told her all about what they'd been doing around Santa Fe and Taos.

"Wow, you've done quite a lot in just a few days!"

"Yes, we have. It's been fun."

"I just wanted to confirm what time you want us at the bookstore today."

"Oh, whenever you want to come. We'll probably go up there around two. My presentation is at three o'clock."

"I can't tell you how exciting this is for us, Charlotte. A famous author speaking here and we know her! The girls were excited when you texted us about it. Thanks for inviting us."

"Well, you're very welcome. I'm glad you'll be there."

They said their goodbyes and Charlotte ended the call.

Good. They would be there. Now, fingers crossed he'd be there, too, so her plan would work.

Chapter 35

The bookstore was full of people when they arrived. She found Zelma to let her know they had arrived. Zelma introduced them to some friends and co-workers and they had some punch and hor d'oeuvres. They found some seats near a podium that had been set up for the various presentations. They listened as a local poet read some of his work and answered questions from the audience.

She looked around and noticed there were a few people with press credentials on lanyards around their necks. A couple were jotting down some notes. After the poet finished, she saw a local TV reporter interviewing him while a cameraman filmed the interview. Good. The press was here. Where was he? She looked around but didn't see him.

A little before three, Debra and her family arrived and found seats near Charlotte and the girls. She noticed Zelma had stacked some of her books on a table by the podium. She decided to go get a glass of punch before her presentation. As she approached the punch bowl, a man standing near it turned around and looked at her. He smiled.

"Hello, Charlotte. We finally meet."

She felt like her heart would beat out of her chest. He handed her a glass of punch and she took it, willing her hand not to shake. There were several people milling about the punch and hor d'oeuvre table but nobody was paying any attention to them.

She turned to leave and he said, "I'm looking forward to your presentation, Charlotte."

She turned back toward him and smiled. "Me, too."

Her response seemed to surprise him. She walked back toward the presentation area and took her seat at the table next to the podium. Zelma was seated next to her. She whispered, "I'm so looking forward to your announcement, Charlotte. I hope it's a new book!"

She just smiled. Zelma stood and walked up to the podium.

"Ladies and gentlemen." A few people quit talking and some who were standing found seats. "Ladies and gentlemen, we're going to begin our next presentation."

Finally, the room was quiet and she had the attention of the audience.

"I was pleasantly surprised when I learned this week that Charlotte Tilian was in town. And even more surprised when she agreed to participate in our event today. Charlotte has a long history with Santa Fe and with our bookstore. I won't tell you how many years I've known Charlotte, because that might give away my age."

A few people chuckled and she continued.

"I'll be as surprised as you to hear what Charlotte has for us today. I'm sure she'll share some of her work with you, but she has also told me she has a surprise announcement for us."

Charlotte noticed Douglas standing at the back of the room, behind the last row of chairs. He was watching her intently. She couldn't tell if he'd noticed his daughter was here with her family.

"Without further ado, please join me in welcoming poet and novelist, Charlotte Tilian!"

Charlotte stood as the audience applauded and she made her way to the podium. She thanked everyone for coming and read a couple of poems from her most recent collection of poetry. She then told them that she was indeed here to make an announcement, but that it had nothing to do with a new book. She looked over at Zelma, who looked puzzled.

"Recently, I lost a dear friend. I'd known her all my life. We were born in the same hospital, lived on the same street as girls, and attended school together through high school. She was my maid of honor at my wedding. I was matron of honor at hers."

She paused, remembering how horrified their mothers had been that she'd been in the wedding while six months pregnant. But Carla had insisted, saying she wouldn't have a wedding if her best friend, Charlie wasn't a part of it.

"My friend was Carla White. I'm sure you've heard of her."

185

She heard murmuring in the crowd.

"But while you may have known of her, you couldn't possibly have known what a dear and generous woman she was. She was a wonderful mother to her daughter, Debra, who is here today."

She nodded over at Debra, who smiled back at her, though she had tears in her eyes.

"And a spectacular grandmother. She loved helping others. I'm sure you're aware of some of the philanthropic activities of Carla and her family. Now, even in her death, she will continue to help others."

She glanced at Douglas. He looked concerned.

"Carla White left me a spectacularly large amount of money, along with instructions that I set up a foundation to help others."

That got everyone's attention.

"At first, I wasn't sure what to do with it. I mean, that's a tremendous responsibility, isn't it? There are so many causes that need attention and I was having difficulty deciding how to best honor Carla. I was wishing she had been more specific."

She smiled. "But then, her husband Douglas gave me the answer."

Now he really looked concerned.

"Douglas. Will you please join me at the podium?"

People turned in the direction Charlotte was looking. Douglas smiled nervously at the audience and made his way up the center aisle toward the podium. She glanced over at Lexi, who mouthed, "What?!"

Charlotte just smiled at her.

Douglas stood next to her at the podium and she continued.

"On behalf of Douglas White and his daughter, Debra Briones, I'd like to announce the creation of the Carla White Foundation. This foundation will begin with two major initiatives. The first is to provide college scholarships for children who "age out" of the foster care system. While many states do provide tuition for these children, as you probably know, there are many other costs associated with attending college. Things like room and board, transportation, books, computers, and so on. These scholarships will cover those costs."

186

The audience applauded and Douglas smiled nervously.

"Now, I told you there were two initiatives. This next one is the one you can thank Douglas White for."

He looked at her and raised an eyebrow, wondering what she was about to say. She turned back to the audience.

"The Foundation will also provide assistance to victims of sexual assault. Counseling, programs, housing, medical care — whatever these individuals need."

The audience applauded again. She looked over at Lexi and saw a knowing look on her face. She had figured it out, Charlotte was sure. She nodded and gave Charlotte a thumbs-up. She looked at Debra and she was smiling and wiping her eyes with a Kleenex. Julio had his arm around her. Charlotte had no idea if Debra had any suspicions about this foundation, and she knew she would never ask her.

A man stood up and announced that he was with *The Santa Fe New Mexican*. "Mr. White, what motivated you to suggest funding programs for victims of sexual assault?"

She wondered how on earth Douglas would answer that question. She should have known, though, that he'd recover and be very smooth in public. After all, he was a pro at this sort of thing.

"Why, to be honest, I don't think I deserve all the credit. Ms. Tilian is far too humble."

Others in the audience began asking questions and they spent the next ten minutes or so taking and answering the questions. Finally, Zelma stood next to her and thanked her for being here and sharing this wonderful news with them today. Douglas walked over toward Debra and Charlotte heard her ask him why he hadn't told her he was going to be in town. He mumbled something about not wanting to ruin the surprise. Charlotte sat down at the table and a line began to form of people who wanted her to sign their books. She had an enjoyable time, visiting with readers of her books and with Zelma.

Finally, she was done and joined Lexi and Jade. Lexi looked over at her.

"Well done, Charlotte Tilian. You killed him with kindness, didn't you?"

She laughed. "I hope so."

"What do you mean, Lexi?" asked Jade.

"I'll explain later, Jade."

Jade sighed. "Everyone always keeps secrets from me."

Lexi and Charlotte both smiled and Charlotte put her arm around Jade's shoulders.

"Don't worry about it, sweetie, it's not a big deal. Are you ready to go?"

"I guess so."

"Let's say our goodbyes."

They walked back to Debra and Julio, thanked them for coming, and told them they were leaving.

"Oh, okay. Would you like to come over to the house?"

She looked at Douglas then back at Debra.

"Oh, no, I don't think so, thanks. We're going to pack and make an early night of it. We're headed back to Houston in the morning."

Douglas spoke up. "It was good to see you again, Charlotte. I'm leaving tomorrow, too. Headed back to Philadelphia."

"Oh?" she replied.

"Yes. I've been away from the office too long. I need to get home and refocus on business. I've been far too distracted lately."

"I see."

So, he was telling her he was going to leave her alone. Her plan had worked.

Chapter 36

Later that evening, she and Lexi sat on chaise loungers at the lodge's pool, watching Jade swimming and playing with some other children. They were sipping on cokes and enjoying the sunset.

"So, I think I get it, but what makes you so sure Douglas White will leave you alone, Charlotte?"

"What else can he do? He can't complain about the money now that the whole world knows about the foundation. He wouldn't want to do anything to harm his precious reputation and hint that he's the awful man he really is. So, he has to keep quiet. Even if he did anything to harm me, physically, it wouldn't change anything. He really has no power over me, Lexi. I've outfoxed him and he knows it."

"You've obliterated the threat."

"Well, practically, yes."

"Charlotte?"

"Yes?"

She hesitated. "He raped you, didn't he? I mean, a long time ago? That's the part of your secret you wouldn't share with me, isn't it?"

She closed her eyes. She knew Lexi had figured it out.

"Yes. He did."

"Then your foundation is even more perfect. I love that you did that."

"It is a sweet kind of revenge, isn't it?" she asked.

"Sure is. I love the irony. One thing really bothers me, though."

"What's that?"

"That he got away with it. Assaulting you, I mean. He's never had to pay for that. It isn't right."

She shrugged. "Not really anything I can do about that, Lexi."

"Are you sure?"

"Honestly, I don't know if I could put myself through such a thing. Making an allegation, trying to prove it after all these years, the publicity…I'd rather just leave it alone."

"I understand. I wonder, though…"

"What?"

"Have there been other victims? I mean, I'd be really surprised if you were the only one."

"I've often thought of that, Lexi. Another thing to add to the list of things to feel guilty about."

"Guilty?!"

She nodded. "Yes. What if there have been others? And what if I could have prevented them by going to the police after what he did to me? Sure, I've told myself it wouldn't have done any good. Who would have believed me? I also didn't want to hurt Carla. Or lose her friendship."

"Lose her friendship, are you crazy? You didn't do anything wrong, Charlotte. Oh, my god!"

She stopped, sat up and reached over for Charlotte's hands and pulled her up, too so that they were both sitting sideways on the loungers, facing each other and holding hands. Lexi stared hard at Charlotte.

"Charlotte. You once told me you had a terrible secret, that you'd done some horrible things. That you were ashamed. I figured you were talking about the drinking, and the affairs during your marriage to Slick Willy. But that's not it, is it? You think you're to blame for being raped. Don't you?"

Charlotte looked down for a moment, then looked back at Lexi. She nodded.

"Charlotte, you were *not* to blame. Don't even think that."

"You don't know that, do you, Lexi? Think about it. My husband had been killed in Viet Nam. He died a hero. What did I do? Spent my time feeling sorry for myself. Then, to make myself feel better, I went partying with my friends, drank too much, and who knows what else? Maybe I flirted with Douglas. If I did, I sure wouldn't remember. After all, I was so drunk, I passed out in his car. Maybe I not

190

only deserved what happened to me, maybe I asked for it. Maybe I was so self-centered, I decided my grief was more important than my best friend's feelings and I seduced her boyfriend."

"Oh, Charlotte. I don't believe any of that for one second. Here's the truth – and I want you to listen closely. You were a young woman whose husband died in a crazy, mixed-up war before the two of you even had a chance to have much of a marriage. You loved him with all your heart and he was tragically taken from you. You were understandably grieving and depressed. Your friend convinced you to go out with her because she was worried about you and wanted to cheer you up. A lot of people in those circumstances would have drunk too much. That didn't make you a bad person.

Then, a predator took advantage of the situation. He knew when he offered to take you home what he was going to do. Your passing out just made it easier for him. What he did was illegal and immoral. *He* is the one who should be ashamed of this dark, dirty secret – not you."

By then, Charlotte had tears in her eyes and wiped them away with her beach towel. "Do you really think so?" she asked.

Lexi nodded. "Yes. But I also think something else. I think my saying it isn't going to be enough."

"What do you mean?"

Lexi seemed to think it over, then replied. "Look, you know all those shows Jade watches about people renovating old homes and making them look like new?"

"Yes."

"Well, think of your life as a renovation project. You've got this old house – it's a great house, with "good bones," as people say. A lot of memories – both good and bad. But it would be an even greater house with some renovation, right? Now, over the years, you've done a little bit of improvements – all do-it-yourself projects. Patching things up here and there. And it looks okay, it'll do, you can manage with the house, the way it is. Then one day, you decide you're tired of the patchwork. You want the house to be spectacular. After all, this

191

old house deserves to be spectacular. It's done a good job over all these years, taking care of you and your family. So, one day you decide to get professional help. You hire a professional interior decorator and a professional contractor, and you renovate."

She couldn't help herself. She smiled.

"But before the renovation, there has to be some demolition. At least that's what Jade has taught me."

Lexi smiled, too. "That's right, Charlotte. Some demo and reno."

"I don't know. What if I don't like the designs? Or the contractor does lousy work?"

"Then you find someone else. Charlotte. Please. Promise me when we get back to Houston, you'll find yourself a good counselor and get some therapy. You need to finally deal with what happened to you. I think this Carla White Foundation you've set up is a good start, and will help a lot of other people. Now, how about you work on helping yourself?"

"You're probably right. I should also try AA again. It helped me in the past. But there's one thing that makes me hesitant."

"What's that?"

"Step eleven. The one about spirituality."

"Oh, Charlotte, you've got that one down. Easy peasy."

Charlotte was puzzled. "What do you mean? The truth is, I'm uncertain about the existence of God. It's a concept I've always struggled with, Lexi."

"Well, the Dali Lama believes the common thread that runs through the different religions is compassion. You're the most compassionate person I know. Think of God as the power of love that connects humanity. That's something you can believe in, right?"

Charlotte considered Lexi's words. Maybe she was right. This concept could provide a way for her to try and practice the twelve steps without feeling she was lying to herself and others. After all, at the end of the day, spirituality was very personal, right? Between her and God, not anyone else's business.

"How'd you get so smart, Lexi?"

She shrugged. "Just born this way, I guess."

They both laughed. "Okay. I'm not so stubborn that I won't admit when someone else is right. I'm sure this old gal could use some demo and reno. I'll try counseling *and* AA."

Lexi reached over and hugged her.

"That's great, Charlotte. And you know what?"

"What?"

"I love you, Charlotte."

"I love you, too, dear girl."

Lexi sat back on her own chair and looked over at the pool to check on Jade. She was still playing with some other children. She turned back to Charlotte.

"So, tell me - did Carla know about what he did?"

"I didn't think she did. But the letter she wrote to me on her death bed indicated she did."

"I just don't understand that, Charlotte. How could she live with him?"

"Lexi, please don't judge Carla. I'm sure she did the best she could. That's really all any of us can do, isn't it? We all have our struggles and we do the best we can. And when we get the chance, we help others do the best they can. Together, we make things a little better for each other."

"Like you are for Jade and me."

She sighed. "I sure hope so, Lexi."

"Well, I know so. And so does Jade. I feel better about my future than – well, than ever. Thanks to you, I think I have a shot at a decent life now."

"Oh, I may play a part in that, but really, you're the one who will create that life for yourself. You know what? This conversation has turned way too serious. Let's drink to the future."

Charlotte held up her glass of coke and motioned to Lexi to hold up her drink, too. They clicked glasses and Charlotte said, "To the future!"

"To the future!" grinned Lexi.

Jade came running over to them. "I wanna do a toast, too!"

The three of them clicked their glasses together and Jade yelled out, "Cheers!"

EPILOGUE

This is Lexi. Fifteen years have passed since that trip to New Mexico. I wish I could adequately explain the difference Charlotte Tilian made in our lives, but it would be impossible. After we returned to Houston, Regina was sentenced to thirty months in a federal prison for violating her probation. Charlotte became Jade's guardian and both of us moved in with Charlotte in her condo on West Clay Street. We had fun remodeling it and Charlotte made sure Jade had space to work on her paintings. We never heard another peep out of Dennis. Charlotte followed his case online and learned he'd pled guilty to the attempted burglary and had received a ten-year sentence. After that, we lost track of him.

Thanks to Charlotte, I did go to college, earned a bachelor's degree in biology, a master's in environmental science, and am now working on my PhD. I head a research department for a non-profit group here in Houston, working on alternative forms of energy. Houston may be known for Big Oil historically, but it's also become a leader in my field and I love my chosen career. I'm married to another scientist and we have two sons, Charles and Martin (yes, named for Charlotte and Marty), who we take to New Mexico for camping trips with their Aunt Jade as often as we can. Jade went to art school in Chicago and now lives in Taos, selling her artwork to tourists. She's practically a starving artist, but she gets by and she's happy.

When Regina got out of prison, Charlotte helped her a lot, too. Charlotte returned to writing and hired Regina as her assistant. They also went to AA meetings together. Charlotte encouraged Regina to go back to school, but she never did. However, she's remained clean and sober, has a fairly decent relationship with Jade and me, and supports herself by working in a flower shop and delivering their flowers. While Jade's dream of sharing a big adobe house in the mountains with Regina hasn't materialized, Regina does visit Jade in New Mexico quite often.

Today is Charlotte's eighty-fifth birthday. Tom and I are hosting her birthday party at our house and the entire family will be here, including Charlotte's children, grandchildren and new great-grandson. Yes, she eventually made up for lost time and grew close to those grandkids of hers. It's a good thing we have a large backyard and the forecast is calling for a nice, sunny day as we're expecting about seventy-five people here today, to help celebrate Charlotte's birthday. She hinted that she would be bringing someone with her so Tom and I are guessing she has a new beau (When Charlotte started dating again, we agreed "boyfriend" just didn't fit when describing these guys in their seventies and eighties, so we settled on "beau.").

Charlotte's back at the retirement home again, after "selling" her condo to Regina for five dollars. She just couldn't keep up with it by herself anymore and she says she enjoys the company of the other residents at The Falls. Believe it or not, she's even leading their book club!

And yes, Charlotte kept her promise to me and found a counselor who helped her deal with the rape. She eventually reached a point where she no longer felt any blame for it. For a long time, she continued to keep her secret, though. Then one night, after Douglas White had been dead a couple of years, Charlotte made a speech at a charity function in which she was being honored for her work with the foundation. Some of the women who had been helped by the Carla White Foundation were in the audience as guests.

Charlotte decided she needed to be honest about her own experience with sexual assault. She didn't go into detail or name the man who assaulted her, but she told the audience that she, too, had once been a victim of sexual assault. She said it had taken her well over fifty years to deal with it, and that she didn't want other victims to have to wait fifty years to feel whole again. She admitted she'd blamed herself for what had happened to her, she'd learned that was a common reaction, and she urged other victims to place the blame where it belonged – with the rapist. She spoke of her gratitude to her friend, Carla, for giving her the means to help other victims, which in turn, had helped her heal herself. She received a standing ovation. I was so proud of her.

The Carla White Foundation has helped hundreds of victims of sexual assault and has helped close to a hundred former foster kids go to college. Charlotte and her best friend, Carla have been a formidable team. Isn't it amazing what we women can accomplish together?

A couple of years ago, Jade and I started flipping houses together. I manage the financial aspects while Jade does all the design and labor. We haven't made much of a profit yet, but it's fun and we enjoy creating new homes together. I guess you could say that is Charlotte's legacy for us – creating new homes. Charlotte likes to jokingly tell others that she was mine and Jade's first mid-century remodel. But we know the truth. She was far more responsible for the renovation of our lives, than we were of hers.

By the way, I eventually chose my own last name – Haseya. It's a Navajo name, meaning "She Rises." A fitting name, I think, considering what I was able to rise above – thanks to Charlotte. I could never repay Charlotte for all she's done for me and for Jade. All I can do is try to live my life in such a way that it makes her efforts worthwhile. And so, each day, I rise.

Happy Birthday, Charlotte!

Made in the USA
San Bernardino, CA
01 April 2018